The overall speed of the convoy had not changed. Glennon swerved again from the road to skirt a crippled APC, and Casca slammed his fist on the cabin wall.

"*Stop, stop!*" he screamed, and was leaping from the tailgate into the sand before Glennon could halt the truck. He picked himself up and ran to the APC. Half a dozen corpses were sprawled about the tripod-mounted Browning. The .50 caliber machine gun was smeared all over with blood and brains and meat, but it hadn't been damaged. Casca yanked it around to point down the road where the MiG had disappeared.

Casca sighted down the barrel of the Browning, pointing ahead of the plane as the pilot flew straight along the line of the road.

Casca was aware of the shots all around him as men filled the air with lead. He also heard explosions, gunfire, and screams as the MiG took out truck after truck.

He watched the tracers and lowered their path until he was pouring a stream of lead just ahead of the plane's nose.

Then he saw the tracers spraying the underside of the plane and knew that some of his rounds had homed. The MiG howled over their heads in its dying rush, its pilot splattered all over his cockpit by the stream of slugs that had plowed upward through his seat. . . .

The Casca series
by Barry Sadler

CASCA:

SOLDIER OF GIDEON

BARRY SADLER

20

JOVE BOOKS, NEW YORK

CASCA #20: SOLDIER OF GIDEON

A Jove Book/published by arrangement with
the author

PRINTING HISTORY
Jove edition/September 1988

ISBN: 0-515-09701-2

Jove Books are published by The Berkley Publishing Group,
200 Madison Avenue, New York, New York 10016.
The name ''JOVE'' and the ''J'' logo
are trademarks belonging to Jove Publications, Inc.

PRINTED IN THE UNITED STATES OF AMERICA

10 9 8 7 6 5 4 3 2 1

CHAPTER ONE

"If I was in Nasser's boots today"—the belligerent little Irishman struck the battered wood of the bar counter with his fist—"I'd put an end to these diplomatic maneuverings and shenanigans. I'd take some direct action. I'd close the bloody Suez Canal."

"He's done more than that, Moynihan," the big Paddy alongside him said quietly. "Egypt has blockaded the Gulf of 'Aqaba."

"He can't do that," a nearby seaman said. "The gulf is international waters."

"Right enough, Britain and France have protested—"

"Nasser's not going to be concerned about Britain and France," Moynihan shouted. "Didn't they try to use the Israelis to take the canal away from him in 'fifty-six?"

"Well, I guess they're going to try again," his friend replied mildly.

The little man struck the counter again. "If I was in Nasser's boots today—"

"And thank all the gods ye're not," his friend interrupted. "The poor bloody Gyppos is likely to be in enough trouble as it is."

1

"And without any help from a scalpeen like ye, Tommy Moynihan," the giant bartender added, and there was a chorus of laughter from several drinkers in the public bar of the House of Glee, officially Gleeson's Auckland Family Hotel.

"And who the hell asked for your opinion, I'd like to know," Moynihan ranted, "you useless Belfast git."

Gleeson laughed so heartily that all 220 pounds of fat and muscle shook.

"And which side might you be thinking of honoring with your services anyway?" he asked the irascible little man. "The Egyptians or the Israelis?"

"And what business might that be of yours?"

"Well"—Glesson shrugged—"you might say I have a commercial interest in the matter."

"And how might that be?"

"Well"—Gleeson shrugged again—"if you happen, for a change, to pick the winning side—and survive long enough to collect some pay—I might manage to get a little something off your tab."

Moynihan slapped the counter in exasperation. "Isn't that just like a greedy Protestant bastard?" he demanded of the drinkers in the bar. Then to Gleeson, "Here we are talking about going off to fight a war to save the world for democracy, and all you can think about is your bloody money."

He emptied his pint pot and slammed it on the bar. "And fill that bloody glass up, before I think about taking me business elsewhere."

"I don't expect to get that lucky today," Gleeson said as he drew black Guinness stout from the beer pump.

"The fat fella might have a point at that," Moynihan's drinking companion said mildly. "The Arabs might pay better than the Jews, you know."

"If they settle at all." Moynihan buried his nose in the

foam of his beer. "And one for Harry Russell too, for Christ's sake," he shouted at the bartender. "D'ye think I've taken to drinkin' by meself?"

"Now ye're getting to the point," said Billy Glennon, another Paddy, built like a blacksmith—the trade he had been apprenticed to, until at sixteen his Catholic religion had prompted him to raise his age and volunteer to save Korea from the rotten Red atheist Communists. By the time Vietnam came around he was no longer a Catholic. "Indade I was an atheist and damned near a Communist too." But there was fighting to be done, and it was a trade he'd come to prefer to blacksmithing. "The Jews'll drive a hard bargain like enough, but they'll settle up all right when the job is done."

"If ever it is done," Harry Russell said as he picked up his glass. "There's one hell of a lot of them Egyptians. They say there's a quarter of a million foot soldiers. And the radio said Algerian troops are heading for the Sinai too."

"I hear you can't get a seat on any sort of plane for anywhere in the Middle East," said Billy Glennon, "for all the Arabs and Jews who are rushing for the place."

"Not to mention," added Harry Russell, smiling, "a few of us Christian gentiles who seem to be heading there too."

"So the Israelis is going to need a hell of a lot of us boyohs," said Moynihan, "and for the longer the better, I reckon."

"I don't know about that," came a quiet American accent. "You can get awful sick of a war."

"All around the bar men nodded. Most of them knew Case Lonnergan, or knew of him. They knew that, like themselves, he had fought in Vietnam. How and why he had gotten out of that war was his own business, just as

each of them had left it in his own way for his own
reasons.

What none of them would ever be able to guess was
how many wars this man had found his way into, wearied
of, and found his way out of.

Years earlier the House of Glee had been the bar where
departing New Zealanders had had their last beer before
boarding ship for Korea and the United Nations forces.
And they had naturally headed for it when they came back.
Later, it became the watering hole and meeting place for
those who had joined the Australian Army to fight in
Vietnam. Other Commonwealth and American veterans in
the country gravitated there too. Many of them hung out
on the waterfront, picking up an odd day's stevedoring
when it was going, and holding up Gleeson's bar when it
wasn't. The rest of the Auckland Family's clientele were
merchant seamen, some of them veterans too. Like the
stevedores, they were either spending the pay from their
last boat, or waiting for the next one and spending the
money in advance on Gleeson's slate. After dark they
would usually move to the lounge bar and their tabs would
grow rapidly as they bought drinks for the mainly pretty,
or at least available, waterfront women who accounted for
the hotel's unofficial name.

The man who had called himself Case Lonnergan when
he was in the U.S. Army had simply walked out of the
Vietnam field hospital where he had been expected to die,
and the U.S. Army had not heard of him since. Captain
Goldman and Colonel Landers, the two doctors treating
him, had found it easier to go along with his disappearance
and lose his file rather than try to explain a near-corpse
that had walked away, or to try to solve the mystery of a
man who recovered from mortal wounds and whose body
showed the scars of having done so countless times before.
And who, for good measure, had carried embedded in his

flesh for almost two thousand years the bronze arrowhead they had removed from his thigh along with all the more recently acquired shrapnel.

In Saigon Lonnergan had found it easy enough to buy a new passport and a ticket to Australia. But the round eyes of the Sydney sheilas were much harder, and their bodies, colder than he remembered from when he had been there on R and R with pockets full of money, and he soon crossed the Tasman Sea to take a look at New Zealand.

In the Vietnam hospital Captain Goldman had heard some of this eternal mercenary's history and would not have been surprised to find him heading off to yet another war.

For his part, the man who had been born Casca Rufio Longinus in the reign of Augustus Caesar had now wearied of the daily round of civilian life as he so often had before. He liked New Zealand and its people well enough but could not get enthusiastic about milking cows, butchering sheep, or felling trees, about the only jobs offered, apart from the waterfront—the same occupations he had avoided centuries earlier by joining Caesar's legions.

Casca knew the pugnacious little Moynihan and his big friend Harry Russell from Vietnam and knew they would be good company to be with in another war. Irishmen had been making their living by fighting other countries' battles for centuries, mainly those against their mortal enemy, England. If these two were going to accept the Israeli recruiter's offer, he was happy to go along with it too. And he said as much. Anyway, it was the only offer he had. There was no Arab recruiter around.

"Me too," a Maori seaman next to him said. "I've been a month on the beach and I don't know when I might get another ship, so I figure it's time to go merc. I've got another reason to see the place too; one of my ancestors came from there."

"We've all got our own reasons," said Billy Glennon, "and right welcome ye'll be along of us Wardi Nathan. I mind your ways from the 'Nam."

Well, that was settled then. They were all going, Tommy Moynihan, Billy Glennon, Harry Russell, Wardi Nathan, and, naturally, Case Lonnergan. They all raised they're pint pots and drank on it.

Like every waterfront city in the world, Auckland had its rats, and a few blocks from the bar Tommy Moynihan came upon six of them. Burly Samoans, about half-drunk and almost out of money, they were delighted to see the lone little white man lurching toward a late-night Chinese restaurant.

"Hey Kiwi, what's a little boy like you doing out so late at night?" they taunted as they surrounded him.

"Me mother felt hungry, and she sent me out looking for a juicy, fat Samoan for supper," Moynihan snapped as he glanced back to the corner where his drinking comrades should appear any moment.

Official histories said that Samoans had abandoned cannibalism about 1914 when New Zealand took the islands away from Germany in the Great War. But it was the standard taunt between the races, and Samoans generally denied that they had given up the practice.

Now there were many thousands of Samoans working in New Zealand, and they hated their white colonial masters even more than the brown natives, the Maoris, their historical enemies whom they had fought on and off for thousands of years whenever they encountered each other in the vast seas of the South Pacific. They assumed Tommy was a Kiwi, as New Zealanders called themselves after the rare flightless, native bird. They gave him no chance to say that he was Irish. He wouldn't have bothered anyway, and it wouldn't have made any difference. With odds of six to one, these rats would just as readily attack a Maori or another Samoan.

"We're hungry too." A two-hundred-pound Samoan chuckled as his great paw enclosed Moynihan's bicep. "But you're not much more than a mouthful for—"

He got no further as Tommy lurched drunkenly, falling backward and pulling the big islander off-balance. As they were falling, Tommy circled his arm out of the Samoan's grasp to bring it around behind his head so that their combined weights mashed the big man's nose into the concrete as they hit the sidewalk.

Moynihan bounced up from the plump back that had comfortably broken his fall to catch another surprised Samoan in the balls with his boot. But then the other four were upon him. Which was a bad mistake. In their eagerness they didn't realize that Russell, Glennon, Casca, and the Maori seaman had rounded the corner. And the first they knew about it was from the pain of kicked-in kidneys and hefty chops to their necks.

Nathan and Casca drop-kicked the closest two backs, and as the Samoans went down they obligingly knocked the other two off-balance. Russell and Glennon were on them before they had a chance to recover, and they quickly joined the others on the ground.

The first Samoan Moynihan had felled got back to his feet, blood streaming from his mashed nose, and got Moynihan by the throat. An instant later he found himself off the ground, one of Billy Glennon's great blacksmith arms between his legs and another under his armpit.

And when he made the mistake of releasing Moynihan, he gave Glennon just the edge he needed to smash him headfirst to the ground again.

Wardi Nathan seized two of his hereditary enemies by their long, thick hair and enjoyed himself bashing their heads together until they collapsed.

Moynihan scrambled up from where he had been dropped and looked about in disgust at three unconscious Samoans and another three running away torn and bleeding.

"A fine lot of friends I've got," he complained. "Here I go to all the trouble of finding these gossoons to entertain ye, and ye don't even leave me one to deal with for meself."

An unfortunate Samoan chose that moment to try to rise and was sped back into unconsciousness by a number of swift kicks to the head accompanied by delighted whoops from the little Paddy.

Harry Russell restrained him as blood started to seep from the islander's ears.

"That's about enough, I reckon," he cautioned. "We don't want a night in jail. Come and have some chop suey."

"Right enough." Moynihan desisted reluctantly. "But pay day first. Lean pickin's I reckon, but these boys has earned their penance. There might be enough here to get us a bit of glee when we get back to the bar."

He was already emptying pockets and removing belts. "We mustn't be going about fighting for free and cheapening the business."

CHAPTER TWO

The Israeli embassy was set in the low-rent district and lacked frills of any sort. To Casca's eye the small, starkly functional building lacked almost everything except submachine guns. And these were in abundant supply everywhere he looked—Russian-made Kalashnikov assault rifles and Israel's copy, the Galil, and Israel's own development, the Uzi.

On the sidewalk in front of the building two New Zealand policemen, one white, one black, stood guard, armed only with short wooden batons. But just inside the high steel fence stood half a dozen Israeli army men, Uzi submachine guns at the ready. The pretty receptionist had a revolver on her belt and an Uzi lying handy by her desk. The two ushers who conducted them to the office of the cultural liaison officer carried Uzis slung over their shoulders. The cultural liaison officer's secretary had her Galil in a clip on the wall behind her desk.

Her office was liberally decorated with Maori wood carvings, spears, clubs, weavings, polished paua shells, and a huge greenstone tiki. The warrior god held an ornate club over his right shoulder, his tongue lolling greedily

9

from his wide open mouth as if he had been interrupted in the middle of a cannibal feast and was happily looking forward to the next course.

There were also paintings of the two unique New Zealand native birds. Neither the huge moa nor the small kiwi could fly and had been easy prey for anybody who had cared to hunt them. The beautiful giant moas had been completely consumed for their meat by the Moriori, the red-haired, green-eyed, brown-skinned aboriginals of the New Zealand islands.

In their turn, the Moriori had been massacred and eaten by the more warlike Maoris, for whom they had been no match. Hunting birds had not equipped them for war with maneaters. The Maoris had been pushed south to these cold islands from their own tropical paradise of Raratonga by the even more warlike Samoans, who, lacking any edible birds or any meat other than fish, had developed a great appetite for the flesh of Maoris.

Whereas the gigantic moa bird had perished, the small, shy, nocturnal kiwi had survived to become the national symbol of the new race that was evolving near the South Pole of the planet from the stock of mainly Scots farmers and Norse seamen who had taken the islands from the Maoris during the nineteenth century, by dint of gunpowder, lead, and steel. The Maoris held them at bay for generations, but eventually their clubs of wood and jade had proven a woefully inadequate defense against the arrayed might of the armed troops of the British Empire.

The cultural liaison officer was young, brusque, and aggressive. Casca took an instant disliking to him but was not put off his enlistment. He was not about to complain if he found that he was going into a war alongside people of this sort of combative personality. He could stand a little neurotic intensity, so long as it was on his side and working for him.

The Israeli army doctor was even more aggressive and opened his interview with the naked Casca by pointing to the great vertical scar on his chest.

"That's the clumsiest piece of suturing I've ever seen. You had an open-heart job or what? We're not looking to recruit invalids you know."

Screw you, Casca thought, momentarily contemplating that he might demonstrate for this jerk just how far he was from being an invalid. A short reach with his left arm would do it, finger and thumb closing on either side of the Adam's apple as he shifted the about-to-die body across the floor and rammed the head back against the brick wall. In his mind's eye he saw with satisfaction the doctor's startled eyes popping as he heard his skull crack against the bricks. But, for sure, neither the Uzi-toting Israelis nor the Kiwi police would appreciate that he was only demonstrating his state of health and martial capacity, and, almost reluctantly, he abandoned the idea. Instead he explained, "I lost control of my motorcycle and had a rough meeting with a bulldozer," Casca lied. "Looks worse than it was. Everything on the inside is original issue."

"And I suppose your face went through your windshield?"

"No." Casca luxuriated in telling almost the whole truth. "I shortchanged a whore and she took to me with a knife." He didn't mention that the hooker's knife had marked him roughly two thousand years earlier.

The doctor almost sneered. "And what about this scar that runs right around your wrist? Looks like a full hand transplant."

"We both know that's not possible," Casca said evenly, flexing his powerful fingers and thinking afresh of a telling demonstration. "This hand works better than any surgeon could pray to fix it."

"I can see that," the doctor snapped, so uncomfortably it almost seemed he had caught Casca's thought.

"Cambodian torture," Casca lied some more. "You ever seen a glove made of human skin? Fortunately my buddies arrived before they got that far."

The doctor produced a stethoscope, not bothering to disguise his disbelief. But his eyes widened as he listened to the steady lub-dub, lub-dub of the heart that had been thumping away in Casca's chest since about the year A.D. one. The doctor's puzzled young eyes searched into Casca's calm gray ones, but then looked away uncomfortably.

"How old are you anyway?" he snapped.

For an answer Casca pointed one blunt finger at the form lying on the desk. The doctor glanced down, looked up again, his eyes flickering over the network of healed surgical scars, sword cuts, bullet holes, bites, scratches, and claw marks that crisscrossed Casca's body.

Irritably the doctor flicked through the papers on his desk. X-ray reports; stool, urine, and blood samples; eyesight and hearing tests. They all tallied with what Casca said, but none of it jelled with the battered hide or the eyes that seemed older than sin.

He pressed a button of his intercom console and spoke in Hebrew. "I've got a guy here, some sort of freak. Looks young enough, but I'm sure he's way past age limit. But it doesn't show up on any of the tests. What do you want me to do with him? He sure looks like he can fight."

Casca couldn't hear the reply, but a few minutes later he was in the office of the embassy's public information officer.

She sat behind a severely businesslike chrome-and-glass desk. A low table held some promotional magazines and brochures produced by the Israel Institute of Engineering, Israel Air Industries, and other Israel enterprises. On the walls were posters promoting Israel's manufactured products. And, within easy reach, an Uzi. She motioned Casca to a chair.

"Dr. Nir says you're older than you claim to be." She stared hard into Casca's eyes, seeking to detect the lie.

Casca calmly returned her gaze. A faint smile flickered into his eyes. "I'm old enough."

"You're an experienced soldier?"

Casca couldn't tell if she had played with the word *experienced* or perhaps it was just her accent. He took in the wide, intelligent eyes, the firmly muscled shoulders, small breasts. He tried to restrain the smile he felt spreading on his face.

As if reading the lewd thoughts that were tumbling through his mind, she added: "Combat experienced?"

Damn, he still couldn't tell if she was playing. "Uh. Oh, yeah."

"You've held some rank?"

No, she wasn't playing. Rank? Damn all these questions. What to answer? Legionnaire, centurion, count, baron, king, god?

Aloud he said: "I've never made general—yet."

She smiled. A good-humored grin. "Our army prides itself that it promotes early and often, and entirely on merit. We don't award medals you know."

"No, I didn't know, but it suits me fine. I'd rather have a raise in pay than a bit of tin on a rag any day." He thought of something he could say in safety. "I made sergeant in Vietnam—for a while."

"Well, that's the sort of experience we need." She smiled again. "You could wind up an officer. But there's one disadvantage—our officers lead all attacks."

"The system I grew up with." He shrugged.

"In the U.S. Army?"

"In my bunch," Casca answered, but his mind had been in another time when the first man on the beach, as the Romans stormed ashore in Britannia, had been Julius, first and greatest of the Caesars.

"Suppose you tell me why you want to fight for Israel?"

Casca smiled. Ah, the luxury of being able to tell the simple truth. Devout Jews believed that before the End of Days their Messiah would come and lead them back into their promised land of milk and honey. The Zionists believed that they could hurry God along by getting there early under their own steam and by building a Jewish sovereign state that they could have all ready and waiting to welcome the Messiah when, at last, he arrived. And Christians believed there would be a second coming of the failed guru he had speared to death on Golgotha. Somewhere in all the prophecies there might be some spark of the truth.

The Jew on the cross had said to him: "Soldier, you are content with what you are. Then that you shall remain until we meet again."

Well he was weary of waiting. Often he felt the crush of the endless years, craved the easy peace of his long-denied death. If only he could close his weary eyes and allow the countless years to take their toll, or if he could fall in battle and not survive to die again. Well, maybe it could happen in Palestine, where it started. Like the Zionists, he was prepared to try to hurry the process, although he wouldn't mind too much a few nights of waiting with this woman for company.

"Armageddon," he said into the lovely wide eyes. "I'm a professional warrior. If this is it, I'd sure hate to miss it."

"Such superstitious nonsense—and you seem an intelligent man. We modern Israelis are not interested in any fantasies such as Armageddon, Promised Lands, or mythical Messiahs. Israel is our homeland and we intend to hold on to it. It's the only one we have. That's what this war is

about.'' She stood up and held out her hand. ''Welcome to
the Israeli Army, ex-Sergeant Lonnergan. We'll start you
as a private. Maybe this time you'll make it to general—if
your superstitions don't get in your way.''

Outside her office Casca wanted to kick himself. Dam-
mit, the bitch dismissed me. Just when I thought I might
have been getting to her. Damn.

The cultural liaison officer issued the new recruits chits
against their first month's pay so that they could clear their
bills before they left the country.

In exchange they handed over their passports. Normal
practice. Mercenaries are always in debt when they join
up. Under any other circumstances recruitment could be a
real problem.

Moynihan's bar tab astounded the Israeli. He could
scarcely believe a man could drink so much. He was even
more astonished when he inquired about Tommy's other
debts.

''What else would I owe money for?'' Tommy asked in
genuine puzzlement. ''Girls don't give credit.''

They had to report back by six P.M. to the safe house, an
old, private guesthouse in the hills on the edge of the city.

Monynihan had no business to attend to other than his
bar tab, and spent the whole afternoon at the House of
Glee. He was raucously drunk when he made it to the safe
house and became much more raucous when the woman
guard frisked him and impounded his bottle of whiskey.
He was not at all mollified by her assurances that it would
be waiting for him when he returned from the war.

The half-heard trill of a whistle penetrated Casca's dream
of beautiful wide eyes.

''Well, I've had worse awakenings,'' he mumbled to
Harry Russell in the next bunk. ''Or am I still dreaming?''

Harry followed his gaze to the doorway, where a uni-

formed figure stood dimly lit by the almost-risen sun.
"No," he said, "I think this corporal is real."

The corporal left them in no further doubt as she blew a
second blast on her whistle. "On your feet fellows," her
cheerful voice filled the hut. "This is the Israeli Army.
We start the day with P.T., then ablutions, then breakfast.
Parade in ten. Roll out." She was gone. The whistle
shrilled in another doorway.

"I knew it would come to this," Moynihan groaned as
his feet hit the floor. "Me ole mither always told me never
to take money from strangers. P.T. she says, and not so
much as a noggin of brandy to get the heart started."

The P.T. parade wasn't all that bad. Five push-ups, five
deep squats, five sit-ups, five chin-ups, a hundred steps
runnning on the spot, five lifts on the parallel bars, five
backbends, five touch-toes. It went on and on. None of it
too tough or too difficult, but all of it just a little more
demanding than anyone had expected to encounter before
they were even in uniform.

Only Harry Russell enjoyed it.

"Just about what I needed," he panted when the inter-
minable series came to an end. I've been considering
getting around to a bit of exercise for a while now."

"So have I," grunted Moynihan from where he lay
exhausted on the grass. "And with any luck, I'll get a bit
more time to think on it."

"Don't count on it," the cheerful corporal's voice interrupted his lament. "After breakfast we double the dose.
This afternoon we treble it. Tomorrow—"

"Don't tell me," Moynihan groaned, "I'd like to enjoy
the suspense."

"And what's the idea of women PTIs anyway?" Moynihan demanded as she walked away.

"I think it's quite an improvement," Harry Russell

said, admiring the corporal's trim, athletic figure as her shapely butt wiggled away from them.

"Yeah," agreed Billy Glennon, "and, after all, about half of the Israeli Army is women anyway."

"*Wha-a-at*?" shouted Moynihan. "Nobody told me that."

"What difference does it make?" Russell asked.

"A bloody big difference. That's all it would have taken for me to join the Arabs."

"Since when are you a woman hater?"

"I don't hate 'em, I love 'em. But how the hell can I make a pass at a corporal? She outranks me."

"Make sergeant," Russell laughed.

CHAPTER THREE

The aging Lockheed Electra put them down at Israel's Lod Airport where they were met by blue-and-white Renault buses with blacked-out windows. Dawn was just breaking, and through the darkened windows Casca could barely make out the glint of sunlight on some parked military planes, a lot of planes. He could not see their shapes, but the bus was moving pretty fast, and the reflections danced outside the windows for several minutes. Quite a few planes. Good. He sat back and relaxed. Plenty of air cover. Very comforting.

Tommy Moynihan had a small radio pressed to his ear around the clock and knew every published detail of the situation. "The United Arab Republic", he informed Casca, "has at least five hundred combat aircraft, mainly Russian-built MiG 21's and Tupolev 16's, the biggest bombers in the world."

"Oh great," Billy Glennon groaned.

"Can they fly them, do you know?" Casca asked.

"Yeah, it seems they can," Tommy answered. "No combat experience, but really intensive training by crack Russian pilots, both in Russia and here."

"And what have we got?" Wardi Nathan asked.

"A lot less, and a lot smaller. A couple hundred French-built Mystère fighters, some French Vautour bombers, and some assorted old British and American planes—less than four hundred all told."

"Five to four against," muttered Glennon. "Well, I've backed a few horses that've won at those odds."

"What about the Israeli pilots?" Casca asked.

"No combat experience, and no special training," Tommy answered.

"Mmm. Well, I guess we'll know soon enough. Is it right about Moshe Dayan?"

"Yeah," Tommy answered, "the BBC confirmed it last night. The Israeli government swallowed its pride and appointed him Minister of Defense, even though he's still the main opposition leader in the Knesset, their parliament."

"Well, he sure did a good job in 'fifty-six," said Harry Russell. "He was a commander in the field, wasn't he?"

"Commander in Chief," somebody said.

"That where he lost his eye?" another voice asked.

"No, that happened when he was a terrorist working for the British," came an answer from further down the bus.

"Stern Gang, was he?"

"No, Plugo Machaz—Striking Companies in English," said Harry Russell. "The Brits formed them to operate behind Rommel's lines. They recruited them from the Haganah, an old Jewish terrorist group from the twenties that specialized in raiding Arab villages. The Brits let a lot of IRA boyohs out of Dartmoor to train them." He chuckled. "But the Paddys taught 'em a few tricks the Brits hadn't counted on, and after the Germans left, Dayan concentrated on killing British policemen and detonating bombs in the bazaars of Jerusalem. They made the Stern Gang look like Boy Scouts."

"True," said somebody else, "but by the time Dayan

lost his eye, the Haganah had become this army we're in now. During the War of Independence in 'forty-eight a mortar burst knocked his eye out with his own binoculars while he was watching a distant battle.''

"Something I've always wanted to do," Moynihan mused.

"What? Get an eye knocked out?"

"No, stupid. Watch a battle from a distance."

The bus took them to a camp guarded by the most ragtag military any of them had ever seen. No two uniforms were anything alike. Soldiers seemed to wear whatever they liked, especially in headgear, which ranged from military caps and steel helmets to turbans and straw hats. Nowhere did they see a pair of polished boots.

A few hours later they had been fed, outfitted, armed, and relaxing on comfortable bunks in a Quonset hut, listening to Israeli pop music on Moynihan's little radio. The huge Billy Glennon was mightily pleased with his uniform, and showed it off to his comrades, modeling it like a mannequin.

"First bloody army I've been in where a uniform went anywhere near fitting me."

"Me too," agreed the diminutive Moynihan. "Me father always told me if I ever could afford it to go to a Jewish tailor. I'm about half a tailor meself, I've taken up so many pairs of army pants."

Harry Russell was delighted with the food. "They might call it goulash," he said happily, "but in my book it's damn good Irish stew with some peppers in it."

They were all impressed with their arms and equipment. They were all brand new, plentiful, and the best of their kind. Casca had just dismantled his Kalashnikov rifle for an unnecessary but ritual cleaning when the door opened and a dark, hawk-nosed, Arabic-looking man entered the hut. The five were on their feet in an instant. They didn't

need to think about it or rationalize it. The three horizontal
white stripes on his upper sleeve said that he was a samal,
a sergeant, and that was enough. They had all been sergeants at some time, and expected to be so again, maybe
in this army. If this guy should turn out to be an asshole
and try to make his rank work just for himself, well there
were ways to handle that. For now he had their respect.

"Are any of you men Jewish?" he asked in Hebrew.

The others looked confused, but Casca had learned this
language when it had been the common tongue of the
people of the Roman territory called Judea, and he had
been serving under the Procurator Pontius Pilate.

He answered for the group: "All of us."

"Cut the crap," the sergeant snapped in Brooklyn-
accented English, "and stand at ease. I ain't the United
Nations—I'm your sergeant, and I want to know the truth.
So far I ain't got a single kike in my outfit."

"Ye've got three Micks, a sort of a Dago with a Mick
name, and a Maori," Moynihan told him.

"And what the hell is a Maori?" the sergeant asked,
looking at Wardi.

"I'm a Maori," Wardi said. "We come from some
islands in the South Pacific that you call New Zealand. My
mother's ancestors sailed there from Raratonga and ate up
the local population, the Moriois. My last name is Nathan, so maybe you can guess where my grandfather's
ancestors came from."

"Well, you might be just what this army needs. But I
don't know if Arabs are good to eat. Nathan eh? Well, I
guess that means I've got one half-kike now."

"And what might ye be yourself?" Harry Russell asked
quietly.

"I'm a Yid. But I'm as much a stranger here as any of
you."

"What's the word?" Casca asked him.

"We could be in action today," was the laconic reply.
"Tomorrow for sure." He turned on his heel and left the
hut.

"A mine of bleedin' information, ain't he?" Moynihan
hissed after him.

"He must be joking about today," Russell mused. "The
Jews surely wouldn't start a war on their Sabbath, would
they?"

Billy Glennon shrugged. "Could be a smart move."

"Nah, they'd never do it," said Moynihan. "It'd sure
be smart, but it'd be sacrilegious, and no Jew would do
that."

"Where d'ye think the sarge did his soldiering?" Billy
Glennon wondered.

"The 'Nam, I reckon," Harry answered, "but he's
damned young. Must have been wounded out pretty bad or
he'd still be there."

"He's got both his arms and legs and all his eyes and
ears," came from Moynihan. "I hope he's got his balls."

"Maybe he's new to the game," said Glennon. "A
different twist that'd be—rookie sergeants and veteran
privates."

"If that's the case, I'm off to join the Arabs," Nathan
declared, and everybody laughed.

By nightfall they were none the wiser, but the hut had
filled up.

David Levy, a fat Zionist from New York, had been in
Vietnam. He threw his kit on his bunk and looked around
in disgust. "Only a year ago I swore I would never set
foot in a military camp again in my life, and already my
politics have got me into another war." He turned to
Casca. "What brings you into it?"

"Money." Casca laughed. "Makes more sense than
politics."

"Maybe." Levy started arranging his gear.

And there was Hyman Hagkel, an Orthodox Jew from London. Hagkel had a full beard, long hair with earlocks, and wore a skullcap. He sat by himself in his corner of the hut, wrapped in a fringed prayer shawl, chanting incantations until the sun went down. Then he burned a braided valedictory candle, lit a Turkish cigarette, and bowed to the others in the hut.

"Please excuse me parading my religion in your living space. A good week to you."

"A good week to you, and a good year." David Levy waved a casual hand. "Your prayers may be naive, but they are not offensive." He swung his feet to the floor to look inquiringly at the cockney. "But tell me, what is a pious Jew doing in a war?"

"David fought," Hyman answered defensively.

"David sinned." The New Yorker laughed. "But what's your excuse?"

Hagkel lifted his skullcap and ran his fingers through his hair. "I thought about it a great deal. I was in Korea years ago, but that was before I embraced Orthodoxy. Now it is different. As a pious Jew, I should not even come to Palestine until the Messiah comes to lead us here. And certainly I should not fight."

He combed his long beard with his fingers, then shrugged. "It comes down to vanity. If the Arabs crush Israel, it will be God's judgment on the blasphemy of Zionism. But also, I will be shamed. If the Jews win, I will be proud."

"The Book of Revelations," said Billy Glennon, quoting: "Vanity, vanity, all is vanity, saith the preacher."

Hyman nodded his head soberly. "Revelations is not reading for a Jew, but the lesson is well said."

Another bunk was occupied by Atef Lufti. Lufti was black and about six and a half feet tall. Thrust through his belt was a silver-embossed leather scabbard with a silver handle set with coral. The curve of the saber was so tight that the silver knob on the end of the sheath almost pointed back toward the hilt. Casca was intrigued to see a weapon he had never encountered before. Lufti understood Hebrew, but spoke it in a unique fashion. He spoke no English; nor French, German, or Yiddish; nor any other language that Casca could think to try him in. Casca pointed to the scabbard, indicating that he would like to see the blade. The black man pulled it from his belt with his left hand, negligently dropping the beautiful sheath to the floor as he drew the scimitar with his right hand. The blade was double edged, about three feet long, and curved almost in a half circle, like a large sickle. An extremely awkward-looking weapon, Casca thought as he accepted it from Lufti.

In his hand it felt even clumsier than it appeared and fell awkwardly out of balance no matter in what fencing movement he tried to wield it.

Atef Lufti shook his head and took it from him. He retreated a number of steps and then executed a number of wide, flat swipes accompanied by some very balletic footwork. In his hands the oddly shaped saber looked graceful and effective.

"*Shotel*," he said as he picked up the scabbard and sheathed it. He pointed one long thumb to his chest and said the single word: "*Falasha*."

There was something familiar about the word, but nobody was sure what it might mean. Casca had an idea it meant *stranger* in some Nubian dialect, but didn't volunteer the information. There could be no benefit for anybody in his revealing anything that might lead to an unraveling of the threads of his past.

From his diary David Levy produced a small map of the world, and the black man pointed to the northeast corner of Africa: Ethiopia.

"Sephardic!" the New Yorker exclaimed in wonder. "A real Jew! I've never met one before in my life."

"And what do you think my race might be then?" the outraged Hyman Hagkel shouted. "Friggin' Arab?"

"No," Levy replied placidly, "Lufti is more Arab than you could ever be. I'd guess your people were Russians."

"Well," Hagkel said uncomfortably, "I will admit that several generations before they arrived in England my people did come from Russia and Poland, but before that they must have come from here."

"Oh sure"—Levy laughed—"we all share that delusion. That's why we're here."

"Speak for yourself," said Harry Russell. "Like Case, I'm here for pay."

"And so are lots more of us," Moynihan added.

"You might say it's the pay," the New Yorker said with a chuckle, "but I well recall a claim that the lost tribes of Israel wound up in Ireland."

"Yeah, I've heard the legend," Billy Glennon said, "but if it's true, they didn't wind up in County Down where my people come from."

"Nor Mayo," said Russell.

"Not Tipperary neither," said Moynihan. "But I guess we're here to do the job anyway."

The Orthodox Londoner grinned and spread his hands wide. "Except the Lord build the house, they labor in vain that build it."

His eyes had the gleam of a fanatic as he looked over the men in the hut and turned to where his valedictory candle still burned.

"We will express the might."

CHAPTER FOUR

The Sunday-morning dawn parade was a peremptory affair, just sufficient to form the thousands of men up in some sort of order.

Moynihan stared around at the motley mob. "Here's a parade to give a British RSM a heart attack," he said laughing.

"Yeah," said Russell, "as undisciplined-looking a bunch as you might hope to find."

No two uniforms were the same. Men wore, it seemed, any sort of headdress that suited them. There were lots of military caps, but many were not Israeli-issue and seemed to have been souvenired from other armies that the soldiers had served in. A number of them, such as Atef Lufti, wore Arab-style burnouses. And, like Lufti, many of the troops carried their own swords, scimitars, daggers and knives. And carried them in an individual assortment of ways, stuck in belts, hanging from harnesses, behind their backs, in elaborate scabbards, or none at all. Nowhere could Moynihan see a decently polished pair of boots.

Their young colonel was a Sabra; one of the new blond, blue-eyed race that had evolved in these deserts from the

Russian and Slavic stock of the early Zionist settlers who had arrived in Palestine around the turn of the century, their religious convictions forbidding Jews to fight and forcing them to flee compulsory military service in the czar's army. Successive waves of immigrants had been forced to flee Europe to escape czarist pogroms, then Nazi persecution. Yet most of these young, blond Sabra officers might well have passed for Hitler's armies.

The grapevine had reliably informed them that the colonel was Yosef Weintraub, and that they were one of three brigades under Brigadier-General Israel Tal.

Weintraub wore a bright-red battle helmet. He had been a Communist in his youth and was still considered a Red by his army colleagues, who called him the Red colonel. The painted helmet was part joke, partly a defiant statement of his politics.

In this parade there didn't seem to be many Jews of any sort in the ranks, and none of them Israelis, but Casca thought that all the NCOs looked like European or American Jews. There was not one unnecessary order or movement to the parade, and they were dismissed for breakfast.

"Efficient bunch of bastards, I'm thinkin'," was Moynihan's judgment, and the rest agreed.

Hymie looked up from his second plateful of gefilte fish. "I don't know if these guys know what they're doing or not. This food is damned unmilitary."

"Yeah," said Glennon, scoffing his second helping of knockwurst and sauerkraut. "I always thought there was some sort of military regulation that the food had to be as near uneatable as possible—at least in any service the British has anything to do with."

"Maybe the French is in charge of the catering," Moynihan mumbled through a mouthful. "They're supplying enough of the arms."

"D'ye think the Brits and the Frogs will be in it this time, like in 'fifty-six?" a voice posed the question.

"De Gaulle has declared that France is neutral," Moynihan said. "LBJ has pledged America's neutrality too, but the Brits haven't said either way. Maybe they're keeping their options open."

"No way," another man answered. "If they'd had the sense to stay out of it in 'fifty-six, they'd still have the canal today. Just arms and money this time, I reckon."

After breakfast there was another parade with the men formed up in small squads of about thirty. The Brooklyn sergeant looked his squad over briefly and singled out a few of them, whom he tried in unarmed combat.

Casca was pleased to see that he was trying out the same men that he was curious about.

He ordered Hymie to attack him with his knife. By the time the succession of lunges and blocks and feints and turns ended in a neat trip, he was satisfied that the ex-paratrooper had not forgotten anything he had learned in Korea. And the squad was impressed with their sergeant as he helped Hymie back to his feet.

"He's had some good martial training anyway," Glennon commented.

"The streets of Brooklyn," David Levy chuckled.

In his turn the fat New Yorker surprised everybody with his speed and agility, and in a second had the tough young sergeant on the ground, his foot on his neck.

"I guess you'll do." Brooklyn nodded in his laconic fashion as he got to his feet.

Elsewhere other sergeants were going through the same process, sorting out has-beens and never-weres, and here and there across the parade ground an occasional man was dismissed from a squad to be paid off on the spot.

In a short while they were back in the hut.

"Well," said Hymie, "this part is like any other army

anyway. You fight for free. What you get paid for is the waiting.''

"And at five hundred U.S. greenbacks a month." Moynihan looked up from cleaning his immaculate rifle. "I'm ready to wait forever."

But the Israelis had a surprise for them. Shortly after lunch there was another parade. This time with full gear and with the mercenary squads integrated with the regular army and conscripts.

Tommy Moynihan muttered as he stowed his little radio in his pack, "I guess we're moving out. Well, I suppose Sunday is as good a day as any to start a war."

They piled into camouflaged trucks with all their gear and were soon speeding away from the camp, heading due south.

"Bound for Egypt, me boyohs," Moynihan chortled. "I've been waiting all me life to see the pyramids."

The long convoy of British Leyland trucks raced along the blacktop at about sixty miles an hour. British-built helicopters flew alongside as an escort and French Mystère fighter planes circled above them. When the paved road came to an end, they charged on into the desert at almost the same speed.

"Do you tink it's started then?" a Dutch voice came from the front of the truck.

"Nay," Moynihan answered, "I heard BBC radio this morning. Diplomatic negotiations are still proceeding."

"Den what the hell for the hurry?" came a Scandanavian voice as the truck hit a bump and sent several men sprawling.

"Ach," a German accent replied, "always these Jews iss in der hurry."

Soon the men were being thrown about all the time as the level desert gave way to the granite wilderness of the Negev where the trucks had to repeatedly swerve around great boulders or skirt steep ravines. But the convoy scarcely slowed.

After three hours they stopped and the men gratefully left the trucks. There were several large, marquee-type tents already set up and inside were benches and tables. Cheerful young women in fatigues and side arms offered them a choice of sauerbraten and dumplings or roast kid and potatoes.

Harry Russell turned to Moynihan as a pretty girl filled his plate. "Ye don't suppose we're already dead and in that great barracks in the sky, do ye? And we've somehow forgotten about the dyin' bit?"

"The Jews is new to the war business, that's all." Moynihan laughed. "They haven't had enough generations to breed the special stock that army cooks come from."

Hymie was studying his tiny map. "Where the hell are we anyway?"

Wardi Nathan pointed to a spot where the territory of Israel thins to a narrow neck between Jordan and Egypt's Sinai Peninsula. "About here, I reckon. Looks like the attack will be in the south, same as in 'fifty-six."

"Yeah, dawn tomorrow, I guess," said Harry Russell.

"There's a huge Egyptian fortress just across the border," Moynihan said. "Al Kuntilah. The BBC says the Arabs have the whole sixth division there."

There were more large tents waiting for them to sleep in, and Brooklyn advised them to turn in early as they would be moving out well before dawn.

Casca and Moynihan walked out into the desert toward where they could see armored personnel carriers, tanks, and artillery and transport vehicles on the skyline. In the far distance they saw a lone jet patrolling the Egyptian border.

"Well," Moynihan said, "I guess the Gyppos know we've arrived."

An Israeli regular hailed them casually as the approached.

"Looks like whole armored division," Casca said.

"Yeah, that's what it looks like." The Israeli grinned. "But if you look close enough you'll see that only one brigade is what you might really call armor." He laughed aloud. "The rest is more in the way of sticks and cardboard."

Casca squinted into the sinking sun. "They sure look real enough to me."

"Yeah, and they look real enough to the Egyptians at Al Kuntilah too."

Walking back to the tents, Moynihan and Casca were rather less than enthusiastic about the ruse. Moynihan summed it up: "There's a brigade of us, and, if we're lucky, a brigade of regulars against the whole bloody Arab Sixth Division. They're entrenched behind some of the most complex fortifications in the world, and we've got paper tanks."

They said nothing to the others and turned in. The last thing Casca heard before he slept was the English-language service of Cairo Radio, "The Voice of the Arabs," with the translation of a speech by United Arab Republic President, General Gamel Abdel Nasser.

Nasser said that Egypt was ready for battle and would welcome a war with Israel.

CHAPTER FIVE

Casca checked his watch as they climbed into the trucks: 0300 hours. Billy Glennon belched contentedly and spoke in wondering tones as he fondled his rifle. "I've sure headed for a few fronts worse prepared than this."

"Most of 'em," Casca agreed, his mind skimming over some of the campaigns he had suffered through. This was the best-organized army of the hundreds he had served in. They could even teach the Romans a few things.

But he decided to postpone any real judgment until he had seen how they shaped up at the front when the heavy shit started coming down. The cardboard tanks worried him. He was cheered to find that in the back of the truck was a five-gallon drum of hot, sweet coffee and another of tea. There was also fruit juice, and a lot of water.

Wardi Nathan repeatedly studied the sky, the stars brilliant through the cold, dry desert air. "We're heading back north," he said wonderingly, "dead away from Al Kuntilah."

A glance at the sky assured Casca he was right.

At 0430 they stopped for breakfast, and as the false dawn began to light the sky the trucks rolled again.

Nobody spoke. Every ear was straining for the sound of gunfire.

Dawn came at 0549 and still no sound. Now they were heading to the west of north, toward the Gaza Strip, the long finger of Egyptian territory that separated southern Israel from the Mediterranean Sea. Planes could be heard in the far distance, but none came within sight of the speeding trucks. They saw only an occasional helicopter, and today there were no fighter plans with them.

The men sat silent, willing themselves to relax. But every man's mind was churning with unanswerable questions. Had a planned dawn attack been called off? Had the whole war been called off? Then why were they following this course? And why the breakneck speed?

Moynihan nudged Casca. "D'ye think our ride to Al Kuntilah was a feint?"

"Maybe. I don't understand any of this."

0600 hours and still no sound of action. From up ahead came the high-pitched whine of jet engines, and occasionally they saw fighter planes circling, Egyptian MiGs patrolling around Gaza, alert against a dawn attack.

0700, and the trucks were still speeding, now headed due west. The terrain had changed from rocks and stones to long, rolling sand dunes. Now they could see the patrolling MiGs in the near distance, but the planes didn't venture toward Israel, although there seemed to be no Israeli planes in the sky.

0740. Airplane engines, lots of them, from out of the west. Casca scanned the sky to the north above Gaza, but the patrolling MiGs had all landed. They had been on the wing since before dawn and were probably refueling while their pilots had a coffee break.

0741. Now another sound as higher-powered jet engines came roaring from behind the first wave of planes. A

massive air armada was heading out of Egypt and straight
toward the convoy.

0742. Helicopters appeared everywhere around them.
From the east, the direction of the capital, Tel Aviv,
another truck convoy could be seen approaching at high
speed. At least a brigade, Casca reckoned, was joining
them.

0743. The trucks rolled to a halt and the men were
leaping onto the desert. Hundreds of trucks arrived, and
flatbed wagons lowered their ramps to trundle armor and
artillery to the desert floor.

0744. Now the first planes could be clearly seen flying
very low in the western Egyptian sky. Maybe thirty miles
away, Casca thought as he caught Moynihan's dismayed
eye. Two brigades of Israeli infantry and armor were waiting exposed in the direct path of the oncoming planes. And
not so much as a tree or a fold in the ground to hide in.
Brooklyn was stretching, flailing his arms about and kicking his legs to rid them of the kinks from the long ride.
Then he unconcernedly opened his fly to piss on the sand.

0745. All hell broke loose. From the west came brilliant
flashes of light, followed by the roar of explosions. The
explosions grew and multiplied. The Egyptian Sinai was
being bombed by planes sweeping in from the Mediterranean.

"They must be coming from British carriers," Glennon
murmured.

At the same instant the Israeli artillery opened up, but
their fire was directed dead ahead, into the Gaza Strip. The
armor moved forward, and the infantry scrambled onto the
moving trucks to advance with them. A wave of planes
came roaring out of Egypt.

"We're sitting ducks," Moynihan cursed as he looked
up at the planes, bombs and rockets gleaming dully on
their underside.

Then he roared in delight as he spotted their markings.
"They're ours. Holy Star of David, they're Israeli Mystères.
Flying out of Egypt? What the hell is going on?"

After a few minutes the trucks stopped and the men
grouped around the armor. A few hundred yards ahead
was a chain-wire fence, barbed wire-entanglements, antitank obstacles, and, Casca felt certain, mines.

Beyond that a dozen or more tanks were burning, the
fires being added to from moment to moment by enormous
explosions from within the flames. A relentless artillery
barrage was raining into the area. Beyond the fence, men
in combat fatigues were running about in confusion. Fire
tenders were uselessly circling the flames. A few Arabs
were running toward the undamaged armored vehicles and
the empty machine-gun emplacements.

A battalion of Israeli sappers were moving toward the
fence, exploding mines as they advanced almost unim-
peded. There was a tremendous noise as the entire squadron of Israeli aircraft came roaring back, skimming the
desert back into Egypt where they unloaded a second
plastering of bombs onto their target.

Glennon shook his head. "If we're moving up ahead to
fight in the Gaza Strip, what the hell are they bombing the
Sinai over there for?"

"Maybe they're taking out the Arab airfields first,"
Casca said.

"Could be," Moynihan said. "There are three big airfields not far inside the Sinai. I wouldn't complain if
they'd spare a few bombs for our benefit though."

The Israeli cannon opened up again, blowing great holes
in the Egyptian defenses, blasting the entanglements to bits
and spreading panic and death among the confused Arab
soldiery beyond the fence.

Casca checked the action of his rifle. A round in the

breech, ready to fire, he moved ahead quickly, waiting for
a chance to use it. He caught a glimpse of Moynihan's
face, alight with anticipation, all doubt and worry gone.
They were about to fight. This was something the little
Irishman understood completely.

A hundred yards now to the fence, and still they had
drawn no fire. Here and there inside the Arab perimeter
officers and noncoms were waving their arms and shouting
unheard orders to the wildly milling troops.

At the fence they halted while the armor rolled ahead
and flattened it, their machine guns cutting great gaps in
the clumps of terrified men between them and the burning
tanks. Casca knelt with the others, and at his leisure fired
at the few officers who were trying to form some order out
of the mess. They went down quickly, and the confusion
turned to rout. In a few minutes there were no more targets
to fire at. They advanced steadily beside their armor,
weapons at the ready, but the frantically fleeing enemy
gave them little chance to use them.

Now they could see the blasted hulks of armored vehicles inside the conflagrations. The Egyptians were among
the fires, cowering and turning back toward their attackers
each time a new fuel tank or ammo magazine exploded.
And each time they turned Israeli machine-gun- and rifle-
fire decimated their ranks. Only an occasional man or a
small group attempted to shoot back, and these drew so
much fire they were almost cut to pieces.

The Israeli infantry and armor advanced in a long,
inexorable line, scarcely able to keep up with the fren-
ziedly fleeing Arabs. They passed the last of the destroyed
armor and Casca counted sixteen burning tanks and maybe
twenty smaller bonfires, APCs and field guns. On the
perimeters of the area he could see other big fires, once
fuel tanks. The fortress headquarters was now in front of

them. Great chunks of the building disappeared as the
cannon concentrated fire on the walls. The observation
tower crashed to the ground, its supports blown completely
away. There was no sign of any defending troops.

Beyond the building the Egyptian Army was melting
into the desert, the frantic soldiers throwing away their
rifles in their frenzy to escape the bombardment.

A dozen Egyptian tanks and some armored personnel
carriers stood undamaged, abandoned by their crews. The
machine-gun emplacements by the headquarters had been
abandoned, too, without firing a single shot.

The Israeli troops moved on, spreading out to cover the
whole of the area until they were approaching the farther
fence of the fortress.

Hundreds of screaming Egyptians were trying to scale
the wire, clawing at each other, dragging one another
down, climbing on each other's shoulders, falling in heaps
to the rifle and machine-gunfire.

Gradually, without orders, the firing stopped. Casca,
like the others, stood still, his smoking rifle in his hands,
but not feeling inclined to shoot any more of the solid wall
of backs that festooned the fence.

Beyond the wire he could see a few hundred running
Arabs who had succeeded in getting over the fence.

Tommy Moynihan cupped his hands to his mouth and
shouted after them: "Have a nice swim in the Med for
me."

"I don't know about a swim," Billy Glennon said as
he gulped the last mouthful from his canteen, "but I sure
could use some more water."

As one man they looked around for some. Suddenly
their throats were bone dry, burning with the raging thirst
that always follows battle. With great relief they saw their
truck approaching and ran toward it, clambering aboard

before it stopped and crowding around the drums of water. Other soldiers came running with the same idea.

Casca poured cup after cup of the delicious, refreshing liquid down his throat.

Moynihan licked his lips. "Better than Dublin Guinness," he said grinning. "I think these Israelis have fought in the desert before."

"You can say that again," Wardi said. "Look what's coming."

A huge tanker truck was rolling toward them, and they could now see many others making their way through the battle wreckage, stopping here and there to distribute the precious liquid.

Their sergeant approached them.

"Good enough," he muttered from one side of his mouth, about as close as this man was likely to get to praise. "Any of you guys medics? And don't say: 'All of us.'"

"Yeah, I am," Casca said.

"You're short of medics?" Moynihan's voice was incredulous. "We ain't got hardly a scratch."

Brooklyn waved an expressive arm toward the piles of Arab bodies. If there had been any Egyptian medics they were now racing across the desert with the rest of the fleeing army.

"Oh, yeah," Moynihan grunted. "Well, I can carry a stretcher anyways."

The others nodded too, and they moved toward the Israeli ambulances that were now appearing in numbers. Only Atef Lufti shook his head. He had come here to kill Arabs, not nurse them. He turned and strode away.

Casca drew some medic kits and the others grabbed stretchers and cans of water. They moved amongst the burned and mangled corpses, looking for signs of life.

"Never did like this part of it," Moynihan grunted as he lifted what was left of a young boy onto his stretcher. Casca's deft scalpel had trimmed away the useless remnants of an arm and a leg.

Harry Russell straightened his long back from bandaging the stumps and looked around. "Well, I don't see no town, nor bars, nor women. I guess there's not much else to do."

He bent again to pick up his end of the stretcher.

CHAPTER SIX

Casca removed the needle from the Arab's arm and patted him on the head. "You'll be all right," he said softly in Arabic. "Your father is proud of you. Today you killed your man. Soon you will sire your man."

The boy's rifle hadn't ever been fired. It lay on his belly amongst the blue-and-red coils of his intestines that Casca knew better than to touch. And he wouldn't live another hour. But the morphine would help him die, and a Muslim who had killed his man in Jihad, Holy War, went straight to Paradise.

Casca checked his watch. It was right on noon.

"The hell with it," he said. "There's not enough morphine or enough bandages in all the world to make a dent in this mess. Let's go see what those Sabra chicks have got for our lunch."

The others were glad to agree. For the better part of three hours, about five times as long as the action had lasted, they had been patching and hauling mangled Arab carcasses. And there were still hundreds of groaning, moaning, shuddering, bleeding bodies strewn from edge to edge of the battlefield.

Tommy Moynihan looked all around him at the piles of bodies and the puddles of drying blood and shook his head. "What a stinking, bleeding mess. Let's get the hell out of here. If I see one more whimpering rag head I'll cut his stinking throat with me bare hands."

"Or strangle him with your bayonet," Harry Russell ventured, and they all laughed at the attempted joke.

"What about this stuff?" Wardi had hold of a stretcher and a roll of bandages.

"Leave it," Casca said, dropping his medic kit to the sand, "for the Red Cross. They'll likely get here in a day or two."

The mess tent was crowded but quiet. The food was excellent, but even Billy Glennon didn't take seconds. Men ate silently, as if in thought.

Suddenly Moynihan raised his head from his plate.

"It could have been worse," he said.

"Yeah, how?" Glennon demanded.

"We could have been with them."

At 1300 hours there was a parade. A few men sported wound bandages, and in some squads a man or two was missing, either dead and already on the way back to the base camp near Jaffa, or in the field hospital that had grown as if by magic a few hundred yards from the battle site.

"Privates Lonnergan and Russell, fall out," Brooklyn drawled, and the two stepped out of the ranks. The Brooklyn accent went on lazily: "Report to *rav samal*, that's RSM, for promotion to rank of *samal*, that's sergeant, and reassignment of duties. Dismiss."

The puzzled Casca and Harry were still turning away when the twang went on: "Nathan and Moynihan fall out."

When they caught up with each other, they found that

these two had been promoted from *turai* to *rav turai*, corporals.

"Dunno what the hell this is all about," said Moynihan, "but it means more pay, so I'm for it."

"I never have managed to work out what promotion is about," Casca mused.

Samal Case Lonnergan didn't get much time to think about his promotion. He now had his own truckload of soldiers to think about, which included Rav Turai Moynihan with Billy Glennon as driver and Atef Lufti alongside him. Samal Harry Russell and Rav Turai Wardi Nathan had their own truck to worry about.

Within an hour almost the entire task force was moving out. The armor was reloaded onto the flat-rack trucks, and once again the convoy was racing across the desert, this time bound southwest, along the length of the Gaza Strip.

"It's got to be Suez we're heading for." Moynihan nudged Casca, who was riding alongside him in the back of the truck.

"I guess so," he replied, "but you can bet your ass there'll be some heavy shit to get through between here and there."

"Yeah, I guess so. This sort of walkover can't last too long."

A few helicopters accompanied the convoy, but still no support airplanes. It seemed that the entire Israeli Air Force had been devoted to whatever was happening inside Egypt.

Mystères and Vautours came screaming out of Israel, flying at top speed, and so low Casca felt he could reach up and touch the rockets slung under the wings.

After a few minutes these same planes came roaring back, again at maximum speed, flying slightly higher, but low enough to see that their bomb racks and rocket slings were empty.

Other Israeli planes also appeared out of Egyptian air

space, racing for their Israeli airfields, apparently returning from successful raids on Egyptian targets that they had reached by approaching from over the Mediterranean Sea. After an hour the convoy was approaching the smoking horizon. Once more a wave of jets poured out of the east, flying close to the ground as they roared across the desert.

"Boy, are those birds loaded," Moynihan gasped as they passed overhead. "It's amazing they can get off the ground."

"Yeah," said a voice from somewhere in the truck, "all that TNT hanging under the wings, plus what's in the belly bomb bay."

"Plus the rockets," another voice added, "cannons, and machine guns."

"Shit," Moynihan muttered, "I'm sure glad it's all going thataway." He sat bolt upright at the thought. "Say, where the hell is the Egyptian Air Force?"

"Yeah," wondered another merc, "we haven't seen a single plane."

"You shouldn't have said that," Casca muttered, and, as if in answer to the thought, the truck swerved wildly from the blacktop as the chatter of machine guns accompanied the stitching of bullet holes in the hood and windshield of the truck behind them.

As the truck slowed and pulled off the road, men tumbled from the tailgate clutching at wounds and yelling in pain. Two or three truck-lengths farther back along the road, a truck disintegrated as the MiG 21's cannon blew it to pieces. And still farther back, six or eight trucks were turned to sizzling wreckage as two rockets roared through them. Glennon still had the truck moving fast, skidding and sliding in the dunes beside the road. Up ahead other trucks whose drivers had also seen the MiG coming were now moving back onto the bitumen. There was no sign of any more attacking Egyptian planes.

Behind them Casca could see maybe a dozen stalled, damaged, or destroyed trucks. Wounded men were hobbling about; more were being lifted from the disabled trucks. Other trucks maneuvered to push the blazing wrecks clear. Two ambulances had arrived and medics were pouring out of them.

The overall speed of the convoy had not changed. Glennon swerved again from the road to skirt a crippled APC, and Casca slammed his fist on the cabin wall.

"*Stop, stop!*" he screamed, and was leaping from the tailgate into the sand before Glennon could halt the truck. He picked himself up and ran to the APC. Half a dozen corpses were sprawled about a tripod-mounted Browning. The .50 caliber machine gun was smeared all over with blood and brains and meat, but it hadn't been damaged. Casca yanked it around to point down the road where the MiG had disappeared.

There was a rattle of steel as every gun in the back of the truck was readied, and Moynihan muttered: "Ye don't s'pose he'll be stupid enough to come right back do ye?"

A bolt clicked as a voice answered: "It's our day all right; that's just what he's doing."

Casca sighted down the barrel of the Browning, pointing ahead of the plane as the pilot flew straight along the line of the road.

Casca was aware of shots all around him as men filled the air with lead. He also heard explosions, gunfire, and screams as the MiG took out truck after truck.

But all of this was happening on the periphery of his consciousness as he concentrated his aim, relaxed his mind, and squeezed the trigger as the plane rushed closer.

He watched the tracers and lowered their path until he was pouring a stream of lead just ahead of the plane's nose. He prayed that the barrel wouldn't burn out, and that the pilot would hold to his track along the length of the road for just one more second.

Then he saw the tracers spraying the underside of the plane and knew that some of his rounds had homed. The MiG howled over their heads in its dying rush, its pilot splattered all over his cockpit by the stream of slugs that had plowed upward through his seat, tearing off his balls, cutting through his spine, the spreading bullets finally lifting off the whole top of his head to spray his brains on the air.

The plane shattered itself to pieces as it slammed into truck after truck after truck, each of the successive impacts of twenty tons of metal and men slowing the plane from five hundred miles an hour to three hundred to a hundred, to a slow-motion seventy, to a sudden halt in a gigantic fireball that took out three Leyland trucks, a couple of motorcycles, about a hundred roasted Israelis, and a fifty-yard stretch of pavement that turned into a bubbling bitumen lake on the surface of which a number of dying men danced about in the grotesque ballet of their last frying agony, to collapse gratefully at last into the boiling black mess.

Casca ran to his truck and was helped aboard by willing hands as Glennon slammed his foot to the floor, and the Leyland hurtled on through the soft sand, past the conflagration, the continuing explosions and the ascending screams of the dying.

Then they were back on the road and chasing after the tailgate of the truck ahead. Behind them, superbly trained Israeli drivers were already maneuvering on the narrow road, pushing away the burning wrecks, clearing access for the arriving ambulances, while other trucks raced along beside the road at almost undiminished speed.

Casca was admiring this efficiency when he heard Moynihan's amazed remark: "Boy, did that Gyppo take some Jews with him."

"Yeah," Casca grunted, "I sure put that ole Browning to good use—for them."

"Well, it's one less Arab plane anyway."

"Yeah. Wonder if they've got any more?"

"They should have," Moynihan answered. "They're supposed to have over a hundred more than we have."

"Yeah, not counting all the other Arab air forces—Syria, Jordan, Lebanon, maybe Algeria too."

"Well, where the hell are they?"

CHAPTER SEVEN

Major General Itzhak Rabin's jeep raced across the tarmac to meet the landing Mystère fighter jet. The pilot, Brigadier General Mordecai Hod, threw back the cockpit canopy and stood on the seat, his head and shoulders out of the plane, both arms raised above his head in a victory salute.

As he jumped from his jeep, General Rabin returned the salute, then ran to embrace Hod as he climbed to the ground. The two generals hugged each other and capered about like pleased schoolboys while mechanics, fitters, armorers, and refuelers swarmed over the plane like the pit crew of a Grand Prix racer.

Hod stepped back a pace, snapped to attention, and threw Rabin a brisk, military salute.

"I have to report, sir, that the Egyptian Air Force is at least eighty percent destroyed.

"According to your battle orders we concentrated entirely upon their Tupolev 16 bombers and MiG 21's, only attacking any other planes when all Tupolevs and MiGs had been eliminated. Almost all of the enemy aircraft were destroyed on the ground.

"We left out radar, we left out missiles, all ack-ack. We concentrated only on airplanes. We flew very, very low. We tried to go around areas covered by radars, or below the horizon of the radars.

"We had three hundred and eighty-six planes in action, only twelve being kept in reserve for our own defense. So far most of our pilots have flown two sorties, and several have flown three."

Hod went on in breathless excitement: "Hey, Rab, it's still only 1115 hours. Let's put the whole bundle into the Sinai now."

"You think we can do that?"

"I'm sure. Look, at Luxor, five hundred miles away, they had sixteen Tupolevs, and we got all sixteen in two passes. Every last one of 'em. Caught them all on the ground and didn't lose one of ours.

"We hit them at all their Sinai fields—Al 'Arish, Bîr Gifgafa, Ath Thamad, Gebel Libni. We hit Abu Suwayr, Deversoir, Fayid, Kabrit, Al Mansurah, Inchas, Gamil, Helwan, Bani Suwayf, Al Minya, Ras Banas, Al Ghurdaqah. And we took out Cairo West and Cairo International.

"There isn't a single airfield we haven't hit. There's hardly a plane of theirs left that will fly. There's nothing left that's worth worrying about."

"Well, we don't know what's going to happen with the other air forces—Syria, Algeria, Libya, Lebanon," General Rabin mused. "I think we should keep some planes in reserve for defense."

Hod's boyish face lit up in a mischievous grin. "Say twelve?"

Rabin roared laughing and clapped Hod on the shoulder. "All right then, you son of a gun, keep twelve in reserve, and put the whole bundle over the Sinai."

Hod was already climbing back into his cockpit, the ground crew unplugging leads and disconnecting hoses.

The engine whined up to peak, then eased down to normal revs. Hod released the brakes and the Mystère taxied away as he slammed the cockpit cover closed.

The whistle of the powerful jet engine rose again to a shriek, and the fighter raced across the airfield and soared up into the blue desert sky, Hod twisting it gaily in a long, vertical victory roll as he climbed away.

CHAPTER EIGHT

The convoy halted about a mile short of the fire and smoke that had been the defenses of Rafah until the Israeli artillery blasted them. Successive waves of Israeli planes were still unloading high explosive onto airfield targets beyond the horizon, while the artillery poured more and more shells into the Rafah area.

Between the trucks and the fires, smaller explosions erupted where Israeli sappers were clearing paths through minefields and concrete-and-steel tank obstacles.

The flat-rack trucks were again unloading their tanks, APCs, and artillery.

Moynihan had found another BBC broadcast and the calm, detached English voice was recounting the day's events. ". . . fierce fighting on a number of fronts in Vietnam, apparently involving large numbers of North Vietnam regular army in support of Viet Cong guerillas."

The disinterested voice went on: "In the Middle East hopes for a peaceful settlement were dashed this morning when Israeli planes launched a series of sneak attacks, bombing virtually every operational airfield in Egypt, catching large numbers of Egyptian Air Force planes on the

ground. Retaliatory air strikes by Syrian planes damaged a
Haifa oil refinery and an airfield at Megiddo. The Jordanian
Air Force has also bombed an Israeli airfield.

"At eight fifteen this morning Israeli troops under the
command of General Tal crashed through the defenses of
Khan Yunis in the Gaza Strip, held by the Twentieth
Palestinian Division. Egyptian losses are reportedly enormous. Israeli spokesmen claim that Khan Yunis is now
securely held by Israel."

"That's us boys," Moynihan exulted. "That was Khan
Yunis we just left."

"There have been some reports," the radio announcer
continued, "of Israeli Air Force raids on a Syrian base
near Damascus as yet unconfirmed . . ."

The rest of the report was drowned out as yet another
wave of Israeli bombers swept overhead and hundreds of
cannon on the ground opened up on the Rafah defenses.

Brooklyn, now wearing on his shoulder the bronze bar
of a *segen mishne*, second lieutenant, nodded to Casca and
his other sergeants, and the infantry moved forward toward
the inferno.

The sappers had been able to work with almost no
harassment from the defenders' lines, and they had succeeded in clearing broad pathways through the outer defense obstacles. With the infantry alongside, the Israeli
armor now rolled through these openings, cannon roaring
as they poured a continuous barrage into the Egyptian
fortifications. Two or three tanks strayed onto mines and
halted, treads blown off, until following tanks rolled them
out of the way. Directly ahead Casca could see machine-
gun emplacements, and with each step he took forward he
stared into the guns, waiting for the muzzles to flash into
fire.

Now he was close enough to see the guns. And to see
that they were unmanned. Instinctively he halted and his

men stopped with him. Brooklyn saw them stop and waved
them on. Casca stepped forward obediently but shook his
head and waved one hand, palm down.

"Must be a trap," he mouthed to Brooklyn.

The second lieutenant cheerfully waved a negligent hand
and shouted back, "No trap. Just chickenshit Arabs," as
he strode forward confidently to step on the first of a
series of connected mines that detonated over a wide area,
hurling torn arms and legs and heads in all directions.

Casca threw himself to the ground as defenders now
appeared behind the guns and the muzzles lit bright orange
as their deadly chatter cut swaths through the attacking
foot soldiers.

Casca hurled grenade after grenade, and the hull machine guns of the tanks opened fire, but all of it bounced
harmlessly off the concrete emplacements while the Egyptian machine guns continued to cut down every attacker
who stood. The tanks were too close to bring their cannon
to bear, and it might be forever before a shell from the
artillery happened onto the bunker.

Casca snatched a rocket launcher from the side of the
APC nearest him and raced forward, Moynihan and Atef
behind him peppering the Egyptian machine gun with
continuous fire from their assault rifles.

It wasn't much, but, as Casca had hoped, it was enough.
The Arabs kept their heads down and their gun silent for
just the few seconds he needed. They started to fire again
as Casca dropped to one knee and unleashed the rocket
directly into the firing slit in the concrete bunker wall. The
gun chattered out only a few rounds and stopped. There
was a brilliant orange-and-white explosion, followed by
some short screams as two men ran a few paces from the
bunker with their clothes aflame. Then Casca and his men
were clambering into the bunker amongst the destroyed
machine gun and the mangled bodies of its crew. A few

yards away the two Arabs who had fled were writhing out
the last moments of their lives as their crisped bodies
flapped about on the sand.

To the right and left the Israeli attackers were hanging
back as they waited for their artillery to take out the
entrenched and mine-protected defenders.

Casca leaped up onto the parapet wall and signaled that
he was holding this gun emplacement. All along the Israeli
line, troops turned to rush for the breach he had opened.

The Egyptian crew in the next emplacement were struggling to turn their machine gun from its normal field of fire
so that they could bring it to bear on Casca's men and on
the Israelis who were rushing the breach in the line.

Casca dropped the empty rocket launcher and ran toward
the machine gun, Moynihan and Atef running with him,
emptying their magazines to cover him as he bit the pins
from two grenades.

All three hit the sand as the grenades exploded. Then
they were on their feet and racing forward again. The
grenades had blown the machine gun apart, but some of
the defenders had survived and were now snatching up
rifles. Casca drew his bayonet, the only weapon he now
had. Moynihan and Atef were out of magazines. Moynihan clipped his bayonet to his empty rifle as the three of
them leaped into the emplacement trench.

Atef pulled his *shotel* from his belt. As he drew the
blade, he threw away the beautiful silver-mounted scabbard. If he won there would be plenty of time to hunt it
up, and if he didn't it wouldn't matter, he wouldn't be
needing it. The closet Arab made the mistake of pausing to
aim his rifle at Casca, and in that brief moment Casca's
left hand scooped a handful of sand and stones into his
face. The Arab's shot went wild, and his rifle was knocked
away as Casca's left arm came down in an overhand arc,
and the bayonet in his right hand came up edge uppermost

to enter the soft belly and rip upwards. The Egyptian dropped his rifle and clutched at the spilling blue bags of his entrails as Casca pushed him away and slashed at the face of the Arab closing on his right.

The second Arab fell back as the bayonet opened his face, but his fist tightened on the trigger and Casca felt the bullet scorch through his side.

Casca turned his wrist as he brought the blade back down to chop through the shoulder muscle and sever the carotid artery to set a fountain of red spurting skyward.

Elsewhere in the trench the other Arabs were fast losing interest in their holy war. The ruins of the machine gun and the dead and dying bodies encumbered them as Moynihan and Atef waded in amongst them, stabbing, kicking, and clubbing.

Moynihan cursed mightily as his bayonet went too far into an Arab and stuck in his spine.

"Give me back me blade, you thievin' Arab git," he roared as he struggled to free the steel, taking care to keep the dying Egyptian between him and his comrades' rifles.

Atef had no such difficulty. His *shotel* was designed for cutting, not thrusting. He swung it in ever-widening arcs, slashing open a throat here or lopping off a nose there, taking off a hand or hacking open an arm. He wielded the engraved blade joyously and gave thanks loudly to Jehovah with each wound he opened.

The confusion of the Arabs turned to panic, and they started tumbling over each other, trying to get out of the trench. Their retreating backs were the sort of sight that Atef prayed for, and his saber opened several men's kidneys, hamstrung some of them, and with one great exultant sweep, beheaded the last man.

From either side of the Israeli front men were now pouring forward to rush through the widened breach.

But the Arabs in the closet machine-gun nests now had

their guns turned from their front to lay down a withering rain of fire where the Israelis were breaking through.

Casca slumped to the ground behind the protecting wall of the trench, and Atef and Moynihan crouched beside him. Casca's side hurt like hell, and he breathed slowly and deeply while Tommy swabbed the wound.

"Went clean through," Moynihan muttered as his exploring fingers found where the bullet had exited. He quickly bound up the wound while all around them Israelis took occasional shots at the two machine-gun nests that had halted their advance.

As Tommy bound the wound Casca could feel the healing process begin. It felt as if the fibers of his flesh were being slowly dragged apart, but he knew that the reverse was happening as the curse of the dying Jesus took effect once more to repair his war-ravaged body.

The dressing finished, Moynihan picked up an Arab's discarded rifle and turned his attention to the worrisome machine guns.

There were now fifty or sixty Israelis in the trench, about a dozen of them wounded, the rest pinned down by the crossfire. Out beyond the line of defense emplacements, the Israeli attack was faltering.

Delayed-action Claymore mines had taken a heavy toll of both tanks and infantry, and the battle was turning to a stalemate as the Arab artillery and tanks traded shells with the Israeli armor, while their machine guns kept the attacking infantry clutching the sand or hiding behind armor. Mortar shells were lobbing back and forth, causing severe casualties amongst the attackers while most of the Israeli shells exploded harmlessly against the Egyptian concrete.

Casca raised his head a brief moment and made a decision. "We'll move ahead as far as we can get into their area," he said to Tommy, "circle, and come back at 'em. No grenades, mind you; we want those guns."

He didn't pause to consider whether some Israeli in the bunker might outrank him.

"Hear this," he shouted in Hebrew and then in English as his extended arm divided the Israeli troops in two. "These men come with me. You others follow Rav Turai Moynihan." He sucked in a quick breath and shouted: "Move out."

He leaped to his feet and ran straight ahead into the Egyptian area, Moynihan beside him, and both of them circling their arms to call the troops forward. They followed, officers and men, as Casca had known they would, and the small contingent raced toward the second line of Arab defenses three hundred yards away.

At the first muzzle flash from the Arab position, Casca shouted to Moynihan and they wheeled apart, each followed by his men, to race along the length of the Arab front, then turn away from the guns to run back onto the rear of the two emplacements that had pinned them down.

A lot of men fell, as Casca had expected, but the survivors were now opening fire on the machine gunners who took just a little too long to realize what had happened. They were cut down from behind as they began to turn their guns, and in a few more moments both Arab positions were overrun.

The few Egyptians who made it out of the trench had nowhere to run but into the rifles of the troops who had been held down out in the desert.

Casca seized the machine gun and swung it right around as two of his men took positions to load and pass ammunition. On the other side of the breach Moynihan's attack had been equally successful and he, too, had turned the gun on the Arab crew alongside him.

Before the Arabs knew what had happened they were being decimated by heavy fire from their own guns. They died still firing at the attackers who were now once more swarming forward out of the sand dunes.

Casca snatched up an Arab submachine gun. With a dozen men he jumped clear of the trench and, firing from the hip as he ran, charged the few stunned survivors in the next trench.

A few seconds more and yet another Egyptian gun crew were astonished to find that they were under attack from their neighboring emplacement.

Now the Israeli attackers were coming up off the sand and charging in force through the ever-widening gap in the Egyptian defenses.

An APC appeared, the young Sabra colonel's bright red helmet exposed about it.

"You, *samal*," he shouted to Casca, "what's your name, sergeant?"

"Lonnergan sir."

"Well done, Lieutenant Lonnergan. That's *segen* in this army. Do that again and I'll make you a *seren*."

The armored car roared on along the line.

Moynihan laughed uproariously. "Talk about gettin' it easy. All you gotta do is take out another five machine guns and you're a captain."

Casca looked after the Red colonel's speeding APC. "You know, I think I prefer the U.S. Army promotion system—they can't hardly make you an officer without asking you first."

"Dunno," Moynihan said, "they sure never did ask me. But when ye make captain, you make me sergeant, okay?"

Casca turned and yelled to Lufti: "You want your scabbard, you better go get it. We got work to do over yonder."

Casca looked across the dunes to the next line of Arab defenses. Three hundred yards of soft, scorching sand, and then a line of concrete-and-steel fortifications protecting machine guns, artillery, mortars. Egyptian tanks were now starting to move out from behind these defenses.

"A lot of steel coming this way," he muttered.

"Yeah," Moynihan grunted, "the Gyppos have got two tanks for every one of ours."

"Well, at least there won't be any more mines now that we're inside their perimeter."

"Yeah"—Moynihan chuckled—"that makes it almost a picnic, don't it?"

Three sergeants, two of them Israeli regulars and one an American mercenary, approached and saluted. A grinning Sergeant Russell arrived, too, and in a few quick words Casca learned that he now had five squads, about fifty fit men, under his command, and that his wounded and dead were already in the good hands of the highly coordinated Israeli medics and need be of no concern to him.

Casca turned to Tommy as Lufti came running toward them triumphantly waving his retrieved scabbard above his head.

"Well, Sergeant Moynihan, do we wait for them to come to us, or . . . ?"

'We're on our way, Captain," Moynihan shouted and signaled to his men, grouping them around an Israeli tank that was moving forward.

Ahead of them some shells burst, then behind them, rather closer, but off to the right, and then closer still and off to the left.

"Jazus," Moynihan cursed, "they're gettin' our range pretty damn fast—and not enough bleedin' cover to hide a pissant."

"Yeah," Casca grunted, looking unhappily across the bare expanse of shallow dunes. He gestured to his men, waving them to disperse. "Let's keep away from this heap of scrap iron—it's only going to draw fire."

They moved barely in time as a near-miss jolted the

tank's tracks off its cogs, and it lurched helplessly to a standstill, slewing sidewise and presenting its largest bulk to the Egyptian gunners.

Casca hurried his men forward. He had been through this scenario before as a Panzer man in the mutual suicide pact between the Russians and the Germans that had subsequently been dignified with the title World War II.

And he had perceived early on that armor offered little real protection, that no matter how thick the steel, it would always be much easier to produce weapons to pierce the armor or disable the machine than to build mobile fortresses that could withstand such shells.

His Israeli comrades in the tank, he knew, were dead men already, and his only present concern was to try to ensure that as few as possible of his own men died with them.

He saw three successive shots from the crippled tank strike the concrete fortress ahead as the doomed tank crew traded shells with the Egyptians. One scored a direct hit and bounced off the curve of the concrete roof of the bunker, another bounced off to the other side, and a third zeroed in dead center at the point where the front wall of the bunker met the ground, exploding harmlessly against the foundations.

He glanced back to see a wild shot from far away, intended for a quite different target, explode in the sand between the tracks of the tank, and he shuddered for an instant at the thought of the high-powered explosive and shrapnel ripping upward through the thin underbelly of the tank. He could easily visualize the scene, great chunks of meat being plastered about the tank interior in a hot, red rain. As the two survivors scrambled out of the hatch another wild shot exploded in the air above the turret. He was too far away, thank all the gods, to see the horror of their astonished faces as the concussive effect burst their eardrums, blew their eyes out of their sockets, and mashed their brains in their pans.

"Great," he muttered to himself. "Three direct hits for the Israelis—no effect. Three near-misses for the Arabs—we lose a million dollars' worth of armor and half a dozen young lives."

As he moved forward with his men, his mind was quietly analyzing the situation. All bad.

In their obsessive determination to eliminate the superior Egyptian Air Force, the Israelis had spared no planes to provide air cover for this attack. A handful of supply and medivac helicopters were the only things aloft.

And the Israeli armor consisted of mainly armored personnel carriers, Bren gun carriers, and light tanks. All relatively fast, but very lightly armored, and undergunned for the task of demolishing the massive concrete Egyptian bunkers, which had been armored almost to impregnability. And now—Casca groaned in near despair—almost directly to his front, a fresh column of Egyptian armor was moving out from behind the enormous concrete emplacements. He saw some APCs, some Bren gun carriers, and a lot of tanks, some British-built Centurions, and many Russian-made Stalins, much more heavily armored and with much higher firepower than the light Israeli tanks.

Casca glanced back at the line of advancing Israeli armor and infantry.

"Well," he muttered, "we've made it inside their outer perimeter, but so what? If this keeps up, we're all going to die on this side of their inner defenses."

The Egyptian guns were starting to wreak havoc amongst the advancing Israelis. For the securely placed Arab artillery, the Israeli armor offered easy targets. Almost anywhere that an Arab shell might land, it had a good chance of inflicting injury on armor or man. Any near-miss would blast off a tank track, or burst the tires of an APC, leaving the vehicle immobilized, its light armor vulnerable to the firepower of the Egyptian howitzers while its small-caliber cannon ineffectively peppered the Arab concrete.

The only bits of good news were that there were no Egyptian aircraft in view, and that, as the Arab artillery was so effectively decimating Israeli armor and infantry, little attention was being paid to his few foot soldiers who were now getting close to the bunkers.

CHAPTER NINE

Casca and his men were now well ahead of the advancing Israeli tanks, but were so insignificant amongst the rolling dunes that they were not drawing fire, not even from the now-advancing Egyptian armor, which was training its guns on the opposing Israeli tanks.

Casca suddenly realized that the men in the armored vehicles had a very limited perception of the field of action. For the brief moment that they were atop a dune, they could see, perhaps, two or three dunes ahead. But most of the time their view was limited to the dune trough that they were crossing at the time.

A hundred yards away to the left, a stream of Egyptian armor, accompanied by infantry, spilled out from behind the concrete. Heavy Stalin tanks were in the lead, then came lighter armor, followed by APCs, and, in the rear, the commanding officer in a Bren gun carrier, all moving at the slow pace of the lead tanks, most of the infantry gathered about the middle of the column.

The genie of desperation fired Casca's brain, and, without further thought, he shouted to his men and turned to run along the dune trough across the Egyptian front toward the armored column.

The sergeants could not see the point in Casca's move, but they followed anyway. For one thing, he was their officer. For another, as Moynihan muttered to himself, what the hell else was there to do? If they kept moving forward, they would start drawing fire from the fortress, and their assault rifles were useless against the concrete ramparts that they were approaching.

Thirty yards from the slowly rolling BGC Casca opened fire, and his men followed suit.

The Egyptian crew swung from their front to respond. Designed in 1941, and improved every year since, the .303 caliber Bren gun on its supersophisticated tripod was probably the most accurate submachine gun in the world. It scarcely bucked, did not ride up and away, but could be held on target with as little effort as a rifle.

Which was just what Casca was counting on.

The first several rounds from the Bren naturally went astray, but the gunner quickly corrected his aim and soon took out one of Casca's Israelis. As his finger tightened on the trigger, bullet after bullet slammed through the unlucky soldier's falling body, and then successive rounds hammered through the empty space where he had been standing.

Casca fired his Uzi from the hip, concentrating its scattered fire on the Bren crew, and giving thanks that the weaponry was not reversed.

The few Arab soldiers on foot who had lagged this far back were hopelessly outnumbered by Casca's men, and all fell quickly to the sands.

The light armor shields of the gun carrier gave its crew something to hide behind, and they made that mistake, only now and then braving the rain of lead from the Uzis to fire at the Israelis; and then only daring short, hopeful bursts before seeking cover again.

Meanwhile, the Bren gunner kept his weapon on full automatic, the rapid-fire weapon squandering his ammunition both when he missed and when he hit, using the whole magazine to accomplish the three or four deaths he could have achieved with a few rounds.

In the instant that the Egyptian attempted the magazine change, Casca and his men were alongside the vehicle, firing at point-blank range.

Atef Lufti again discarded his precious silver scabbard. He wielded the *shotel* in a great overhand arc, reaching over the side armor and beyond the man nearest to him, to take the driver through the chest, the point of the steeply curved scimitar entering through the man's heart to emerge through his back in the region of his kidneys.

The officer next to the driver fired his pistol in all haste, but the side armor shield was between him and Lufti. The bullet ricocheted from the steel, the flash and the explosion at such immediate range disconcerting him just long enough for Atef to recover his *shotel*. The razor-sharp outer edge effortlessly sliced open the officer's throat as Atef withdrew it backhand from the driver's chest. And he continued the round-arm sweep to hack open the throat of one of the men by the Bren gun in the center of the vehicle.

Casca, Glennon, and a number of others were clambering over the armored tailgate, shooting at point-blank range, clubbing, stabbing, punching, and kicking as they eliminated the crew and took over the vehicle.

Billy Glennon booted the dying driver from his seat, giving thanks that his body had protected the controls and wiring from all the flying lead.

He flopped happily into the seat and was wrenching the wheel around to swerve away from the Egyptian line when Casca shouted: "Let's take these in front before we leave."

At the trigger of the Bren, Moynihan was ready to comply. He switched the weapon to semiautomatic and fired rapidly into the backs of the men in the APC ahead. Elevating the barrel slightly, he wreaked similar butchery on those in the APC climbing the farther face of the dune. With the accompanying fire from half a dozen Uzis, the entire personnel of both APCs was accounted for.

Casca tapped Glennon on the shoulder and motioned him to back up.

Three vehicles ahead, another APC was dipping down into the next dune trough, its crew not even dimly aware of what had happened to their following comrades. Nor, amid all the mayhem, had they any real idea of where the fire was coming from. Nor had the Arab defenders in the bunkers realized that their two APCs had been knocked out by one of their own BGCs. Their attention, along with their gun sights, was concentrated on the distant broad line of advancing Israeli attackers.

The reversing BGC raced backward through the opening in the concrete ramparts, Billy Glennon whooping in delight as one foot gunned the motor, his body twisted around to face the direction they were heading, one hand behind him effortlessly steering as if at the helm of a boat.

If the nearby Egyptians thought about it at all, they only saw that two of their APCs had been wiped out, and that the command vehicle was retreating to safety. Their first inkling that this was not the case came as the Bren opened up on their backs, and by then it made no difference what they thought.

Before the last of the surprised Arabs fell, Billy Glennon skidded to a halt and Atef and the others were tumbling into the bunkers to drag the dying bodies away from the guns. Then Glennon was changing into forward gear again, Moynihan at the Bren, half a dozen others with Uzis wreaking similar havoc upon the bunker on the other side of the opening while Wardi Nathan led the rest of Casca's platoon in through the undefended gap in the Egyptian line. Harry Russell got behind an Arab cannon and cranked it down until he had brought the sights from the distant Israeli attack force to the much closer Egyptian defenders moving out to meet the advancing Jews.

"Somebody load for me," he shouted, and two Israelis leaped to comply.

His first few shots fell short, but then he came close enough to APC for the concussive effect of the bursting shell to blow out the tires.

"That's fancy cannon shooting for an infantryman," Casca said in some surprise.

Harry ignored the wobbling wreck as he brought up the sights to aim at the next vehicle, a light tank.

"I got me start in artillery," he said, and three or four shots later he came close enough to displace a track and the tank ground to a halt.

His sights searched greedily for another tank, and this time he quickly scored a hit, the armor-piercing shell penetrating the tank's turret wall, sending shards of the hot, torn steel flying about inside the confines of the cabin, tearing through bodies, severing limbs, smashing skulls.

The gun sights roved on along the line, Casca motioning to him to try for the farthest target, the lead Egyptian tank. Harry readily complied with Casca's order, moving up the gun barrel along the line of Egyptian tanks, but continuing his fire. Each successive shot landed somewhere along the line of enemy armor, every so often one of them taking effect on either the machines or the accompanying infantry.

Then the heavy, British-built Centurion was in his sights, and he was bouncing round after round off its thick armored hide.

But even the thickest steel is no match for high explosive, and soon the Egyptian column was fanning out to avoid the smoking wreck of the Centurion.

Now Wardi Nathan and Atef Lufti had a recoilless rifle

firing from the adjacent bunker, and the two guns between them took heavy toll of the Egyptian armored column.

Billy Glennon stationed the Bren gun carrier to the rear of the two conquered bunkers, and the men on board were able to quickly wipe out the handful of Egyptians who attempted to rush the bunkers when they realized what had taken place. Each bunker was equipped with a number of machine guns, and these, too, were now turned to their rear as more and more Arab troops tried to take back the captured positions. But the Egyptians had left few infantry in reserve behind the gun emplacements, and these few were spread thinly all along the line.

The Israeli troops had been ordered always to concentrate their fire on officers and NCOs, and as each charge on the bunkers failed, the retreating rabble of unblooded young boys served to spread confusion and terror amongst the succeeding groups of Arab youth.

Some of the younger officers, and even some of the noncoms, caught the contagion of fear, and the two bunkers were soon secure, the Egyptians only firing at them from a small distance from the protection of other bunkers, or from behind the next dune line.

Out in the general battlefield, the two lines of armor had now met, and men and machines were milling about in a confusion of explosions, smoke, screams, and gunfire. The confusion grew as Egyptian tanks turned to chase Israeli armor that had broken through their lines, and some of the Israeli tanks swerved back to protect the rear of their main attacking force.

Harry Russell shook his head to Casca as he stopped firing his cannon.

"Can't tell who I might hit," he shouted.

Casca nodded. The mix-up of camouflaged armor was all the greater, because both sides were using many vehicles of the same make. British, French, Russian, U.S., and Czech armor were milling about in a hideous cocktail of noise and death

"Spike it," Casca shouted, and Russell quickly destroyed the cannon's firing mechanism.

Casca shouted to where Moynihan's crew were keeping the Arab infantry busy from within the Bren carrier's protective armor.

Glennon put down his Uzi and jumped into the driver's seat, backing to the edge of the bunker. Every man that the vehicle could carry clambered aboard and Billy gunned the car out into the dunes behind the bunkers, then brought it back in a tight curve aimed at the rear of the nearest bunker still held by the Egyptians.

At the same time, Wardi Nathan's men were pouring machine-gun fire into the bunker from their position.

Outnumbered and under attack from two directions, the hapless Egyptians were offered the chance to die neither bravely nor well, but only quickly.

If all the reserve Arab infantry had just then rushed the captured bunkers, they might well have dislodged the Israelis. But they lacked both the will and the leadership, and as Casca repeated the tactic on yet another bunker even this opportunity evaporated.

An Israeli officer produced a flag and stood atop the bunker waving it.

"Come down, you stupid fool," Casca shouted at him, but the young Sabra shook his head and died with a delighted grin on his face as he was almost cut in two by Egyptian gunfire.

But the blue and white bars and the Star of David had been seen, and the Israeli troops out in the field made a concerted rush for the occupied part of the Arab defenses. They ran into heavy fire from Egyptian machine gunners and a huge number died, but many more made it into the captured bunkers, and the flag was quickly raised again, this time on a rifle wedged in a gun slot.

The breach in the Egyptian line widened as bunker after bunker was overrun. And suddenly the Egyptian defense was dissolving in the same sort of leaderless, mindless panic that had happened at Khan Yunis.

The Red Colonel's armored car came racing through the breach. It didn't pause, but the colonel waved his bright red battle helmet and shouted: "Well done, *Rav Seren*. You're a major now. Keep it up. Get your men watered and fed. I've got a company for you to command." He waved his red helmet again and clapped it back on his blond head. "On to Al 'Arish." The armored car was racing away along the line.

Water.

Casca realized that he had emptied his canteen in a few greedy gulps. He could sure use some water. As the thought struck him he heard a delighted yelp from Moynihan.

"Oh boy, here comes the water wagon!" And he saw several big tanker trucks approaching so close to the action that they were passing some of the fleeing Arab soldiers.

CHAPTER TEN

Casca found Colonel Weintraub's headquarters in what had been the Egyptian command post. The young Sabra had been promoted to full colonel and now had under his command a regiment of five battalions, a total of two thousand men. He greeted Casca warmly. "Well, Major, how do you like the way this army operates?"

"Suits me fine." Casca laughed. "I'm not thinking of resigning my commission."

"Can't be done." The colonel laughed in reply. "That is one item where we didn't copy the British. Israeli officers do not have that privilege. In our book, an officer's resignation in wartime is desertion and is treated accordingly."

"In fact," said Casca, "I see that, in this army, officers don't enjoy too many privileges."

The colonel shook his blond head. "In this army what officers enjoy is responsibility."

"Okay with me."

The Sabra appraised Casca shrewdly. "You've held command before, haven't you?"

"Some."

"Care to tell me?"

"It would take some time, and I doubt you have much to spare."

"None at all. We're pushing right on to Al 'Arish. And I don't give a damn anyway. For all I care you might have been with Hitler. You know how to fight, and that's what we need."

Casca nodded. Jews were a generally practical people. But he smiled to himself as he thought that after this was over he just might tell Weintraub something of his history. It didn't seem quite the time now to mention that he had, in fact, fought for Hitler.

Weintraub led him to a large-scale map on the wall. The Gaza Strip looked ridiculously tiny on the northeast corner of the enormous Sinai Peninsula, which separated it from the Gulf of Suez, the canal, and beyond that, the still-much-greater expanse of Egypt proper.

The so-far-victorious Israeli Army had in hard fact barely succeeded in inflicting a flea bite on an insignificant outpost of the United Arab Republic.

Weintraub's hand spread over the Sinai. "As you can see, we have a little way to go. This wasteland of rock and desert, the Sinai, is where my ancestors, don't ask me why, wandered with Moses for forty years. We must take it all.

"There are seven Egyptian divisions, something like a hundred thousand men, enormous numbers of artillery, and about a thousand tanks to prevent us."

He laid a slim finger on the map. Where his whole hand had been widely extended to encompass the Sinai, his one finger covered all of Israel and a big chuck of Jordan. To the north lay Lebanon, to the east Syria and the rest of Jordan, to the south the huge deserts of Saudi Arabia.

"We are two and a half million people set amongst these

countless millions of Arabs. Some of us, like myself, have never known any other homeland. Others have been dispossessed from Germany, Poland, Russia, and the rest of Europe, or have come here voluntarily from the United States, other countries, even China.

"We have nowhere else to go, nowhere to run to, nowhere to hide, other than this tiny sliver of sand and stone, only nine miles wide at the waist, that we call Israel. We have to win; we have no alternative."

He grinned. "Fortunately, our millions of enemies do have an alternative—they can learn to leave us alone."

The grin widened. "It is our job, yours and mine and our comrades', to teach them that they must leave us alone." He pointed to the south of Al 'Arish. "My C.O., General Yeshayah Gavish, is in command of this front. We are in three task forces, which include most of the armored strength of Israel. This armor is outnumbered two to one by Egyptian armor—and theirs is in no way inferior, mainly Centurions and brand-new Stalins. Ours, as you have seen, are a few Centurions, some old Pattons, and a lot of antiquated Shermans. We must knock out every possible enemy tank, and I already see that you need no instruction on that score. We are Task Force One, and it is our job to make the breakthrough at Al 'Arish.

"Here, at Abu Agheila"—his finger stabbed the map not far from the Israel-Egypt border—"is the enormous complex of fortifications that commands the central axis through the Sinai. Our General Sharon is moving on it now with Task Force Two.

"Meanwhile our General Yoffe with Task Force Three is heading across the trackless sand dunes between Al 'Arish and Abu Agheila to cut off any reinforcement of Al 'Arish from that direction. The Egyptians have left this waterless wasteland undefended because they consider it impassable. And, who knows, they may be right. If my good friend Avraham Yoffe makes it, he will set up a blocking position at Bîr al Lahtan.''

Casca looked at the enormous area of the Arab territories, the small slice that was Israel, and the minuscule portion of the Gaza Strip that they had occupied.

''Well''—he shrugged—''the day is young yet.''

''Yes,'' the colonel replied, ''we should be on the outskirts of Al 'Arish by nightfall.'' The cheerful grin again lit up his young face. ''Fortunately we Israelis have learned to be specialists in night action—our army, the Zahal, grew out of the Haganahir and the Night Squads with which we terrorized Palestinian villages during the twenties and thirties. They were developed and trained by a British officer, Orde Wingate, and he did a damned good job.''

Casca nodded. ''I've had a few fights in the dark myself.''

Within the hour Casca's company was on the move. His casualties had been replaced again, and he now had under his command four platoons of foot soldiers and a heavy weapon squad well equipped with machine guns and mortars.

While Samal Harry Russell drove, Samal Tommy Moynihan sat in the rear seat twiddling the dial of his transistor radio and picking up reports of the war from Radio Cairo, the BBC, Israel Radio, Voice of America, and Radio Jordan.

Some of the reports conflicted, but, piecing together the various viewpoints it seemed that Syrian planes had attacked a Haifa oil refinery and an airfield at Megiddo. The Jordanian Air Force had bombed an Israeli airfield. In retaliation the Israeli Air Force, which seemed to be everywhere except where Moynihan would have wished—overhead—had attacked the main Syrian air base near the capital city of Damascus, and the biggest of Jordan's air bases. In both cases, as in the earlier attacks on Egypt, the Israeli fliers had surprised the Arab air forces on the ground and wreaked near-total destruction.

But at Al 'Arish there was to be no element of surprise. The Egyptian 20th Palestinian Division had lost fifteen hundred men and countless thousands were wounded in the battle for Rafah on the Gaza Strip. Al 'Arish would be the first battle in the strategically vital Sinai, and the Egyptians were determined not to lose it. They were well prepared, well warned, and ready and waiting when the Israeli vanguard came upon the post's outer fortifications as the sun was setting.

"Oh, b'Jazus," Harry Russell groaned from behind the wheel as Casca's jeep topped the last rise, "this is going to be even worse than I thought."

"Yeah," Casca grunted, "the sun is sure not going to help us too much."

The great, golden orb was glaring directly into the windshield so that they could scarcely see their objective. The Arabs, on the other hand, had the sun at their backs, spotlighting and almost blinding their attackers while they blended into long shadows.

Israeli ambulances were rushing back and forth to where sappers were at work, trying to detonate pathways through the minefields. From the distance Arab gunners were having a field day, pouring heavy fire onto the sappers, who were suffering enormous casualties.

The Israeli artillery was searching for the Egyptian guns, but were probing blind without recon information from aircraft. Now fresh Arab fire opened up, reaching for where Casca and the rest of Colonel Weintraub's regiment had arrived in sight. To be sure, the shells were all falling short, but the Egyptian gunners would soon get that right. Besides, the Israelis had to advance into their guns anyway.

"Where's our fucking air cover?" Moynihan fumed.

"Feels just like 'fourteen," Casca muttered, almost to himself, "when we didn't have any planes."

"I thought you were older than me," Harry Russell said, chuckling, "but I didn't think you were that old."

Casca bit his tongue. Yes, he had been thinking of his time in the Great War when the only aircraft had been the rare reconnaissance patrols. Got to watch that.

Suddenly the war was updated as a squadron of French-built Vautour bombers appeared out of the Israeli sky. Flying almost on the ground, they swooped on the Egyptian guns and took the heat off the sappers.

A flight of Mystère fighters screamed overhead, coming in, it seemed, just feet off the ground, avoiding all possible detection by the Egyptians. The Arabs heard the engines and the cannon of the Mystères at about the same time, and the effect was devastating and demoralizing.

One moment the Arabs had the field to themselves, plastering the Israeli sappers at will and laying down a barrage of discouragement for Casca's men. One moment more, and they were cowering amongst the wreckage of their guns.

"Well," came the voice of Moynihan in the back of the jeep, "things is improving a bit in the air anyway."

"But where is the Egyptian Air Force?" demanded a puzzled Harry Russell.

"Retired hurt is what we call it in Rugby," said Moynihan.

"Sure, but they can't be that bad hurt—can they?"

The Vautours came back in another pass, unloading another rain of death on the Arab gunners. The sappers made good use of the respite, their practiced eyes now discerning the inevitable pattern in the distribution of the mines. All mine layers strove to avoid any regularity, and the harder they tried the more clearly the pattern showed once sufficient mines were detected.

From his vantage point atop a twenty-foot dune, Casca saw the pattern, too, and discerned the safe, or anyway half-safe, track through the minefields.

"Let's go," he said without thinking about it further. "The sooner we get there the sooner we're through with it."

Billy Glennon seemed fired by the same idea and had his foot hard down on the accelerator almost before Casca finished speaking. The trucks charged forward to keep pace behind Casca's jeep.

"Any idea where you're going?" Casca shouted to Billy. Glennon shot him a quick, worried glance, then returned his attention to what the sappers had accomplished ahead of them.

"I thought I saw the safe line," Billy said, a tinge of uncertainty in his voice. "Didn't ye?"

Casca laughed and hoped his voice sounded confident. "Yeah, we're going right—I hope."

But had his seat in the jeep permitted it, Casca would have been kicking himself in the butt.

"Let's go," was easy enough to say. If you happened to be a major leading a company of combat-experienced, disciplined troops, it was just as sure that they would follow. But where the hell were they going? And what were they going to do when they got there?

Casca shrugged off the thought. From the first he had never really understood too well what he was doing as he went into battle, and two thousand years of experience had not enlightened him.

"Let's go. Let's go. Let's go." His repeated shout was taken up by everybody in the jeep, and then by all of the others.

There was a tremendous explosion behind them as one of Casca's drivers strayed a few yards from Billy's lead and encountered a mine.

"Keep going," Casca shouted, looking back.

The disaster was already under control. The following truck had stopped and its troops were already pulling wounded from the wreckage. Two ambulances were racing for the position. The other trucks had deviated gingerly in single file to avoid the wreck, and were now back on the tail of Casca's jeep and catching up fast.

Farther back Casca saw tanks, APCs, and trucks full of infantry rushing to follow his lead. Colonel Weintraub's red helmet was in the lead armored car.

Glennon twisted for a moment in his seat as he heard a tank find another mine.

"One thing," he gritted between clenched teeth, "every one we find is one less to look for."

"Yeah." Casca tried to laugh but it didn't quite work. He had lost quite a few men. He wasn't going to think about who they might have been or how close they were to him. Whoever they were they were now lying in assorted bleeding pieces behind him, and, who knew, maybe this was a half-assed maneuver anyway.

A junior field officer with a few infantry in open trucks and jeeps leading an armored attack on an extremely well-protected fortress was not just unconventional, it might well prove suicidal. But they were well and truly committed now.

What the maneuver had achieved was an astonishing turn of speed. They were now passing the last of the sappers and they left the minefield for the home ground of the defenders. Casca signaled and his trucks fanned out to either side of the jeep as Billy Glennon increased speed. Some way behind Casca's company came Colonel Wein-

traub's armored car, and he too was signaling to his infantry trucks to move up ahead of the armor.

Casca offered a little prayer to Mars. He knew well that
the very worst ideas could be just as contagious as the best
ones. History was littered with graveyards to prove it with
names like Balaclava, Gallipoli, Stalingrad, Arnhem, and
he had personally experienced several of them.

They were now close to some Egyptian artillery and
machine-gun emplacements. The Vautours' bombs and the
Mystères' cannon had turned these bunkers to ruins in a
few brief seconds. But the destruction had not been total.
Casca could see men running about trying to haul guns
back into firing positions.

He looked over his shoulder. They had far outdistanced
the rest of the Israeli attack. Casca's company was out on
its own.

Farther back the other trucks full of infantry were fanning out across the desert, and, way back were the slow-
moving armored vehicles. The Red colonel's armored car,
its engine no doubt close to disintegration, was keeping
pace with the second wave of infantry trucks.

As he watched, Casca saw the blond head as Weintraub
snatched off his red helmet and waved it in an unmistak-
able signal. "Let's go," Casca yelled, and again his troops
took up the shout.

They raced forward, two hundred throats shouting: "Let's
go. Let's go. Let's go."

They were still shouting as the Egyptian machine guns
opened up and Casca brought the vehicles to a halt. Leaping from the jeep before it stopped, he ran forward, shouting into the guns, two hundred screaming devils with him,
all yelling in a frenzy: "*Let's go! Let's go! Let's go!*"

The sun was now a blazing disc on the edge of the
desert. The Arabs were trying to collect themselves in
the shadows, blundering about in the half dark amidst the

broken guns and bodies, twisted steel and concrete. To their front, lit blood red by the setting sun, came a host of screaming crazies armed with nothing but small assault rifles, but getting closer, terrifyingly closer, every second.

And behind these crazies there now were dozens of other trucks spilling hundreds more infantry onto the sand and they were all racing forward screaming.

And, farther back still, outlined against the darkening sky, the whole horizon was spread with the red silhouettes of Israeli tanks.

And, in the middle ground was a racing armored car, turret open, a blond head and red helmet waving like a battle flag.

It was too much.

In fact, the Arab machine guns were killing a lot of Casca's men, and, in cooler hands, might have killed all of them. But, in the bunkers, among the groans of the dying, the screams of the wounded, the stench of blood and piss and shit and cordite and petrol, there were no cool heads. Every Egyptian had alongside him a corpse or a moaning, dying comrade. And from out of the desert more death was coming in an endless, blood-red wave.

A few Arabs had second thoughts about their Jihad, and their hands faltered at the guns. Their rate of fire slackened. They couldn't see the numbers of the attackers who fell. The sun only lit the ones on their feet, getting closer and closer, and now pouring fire into the bunkers.

As the first of the attackers' bullets took effect, the defenders stopped firing. They stood and backed away from their smoking weapons and the screaming remains of their friends. Then more of them were falling to the hail of fire from Casca's men, and the Arabs broke and ran.

As in most armies, Egyptians officers led from the rear, only young boy subalterns being with the troops in the first line of fire.

Subaltern, NCO, or private, by now all the heroes were dead, and the wave of terrified humanity that was pouring back out of the gun emplacements was through with any idea of heroics.

The Jihad, the Holy War that guaranteed eternal Paradise for those who died in it, was no longer of interest to any of these men.

Having your testicles torn off, your guts ripped out, your own leg blown clear of your body to have your falling boot kick you in the head, to taste the bitterness of your own waste as you fell face down into the mess of your dangling intestines—these were too high a price to pay for Paradise. There must be a better means to get there or else Paradise was going to be very sparsely populated.

The officers at the rear were overwhelmed by their retreating troops, and, no matter how they felt about it, were swept back in the retreating wave or simply trampled underfoot.

All along the line of the Egyptians defense, man's most powerful emotion spread like a brushfire. Sheer terror swept the line and mindless panic ensued.

Here and there among the defenders a cool head prevailed, and some of the Israelis met fierce resistance, but by the time darkness fell most of the outer defenses of Al 'Arish had fallen.

Not even David Levy, nor the most devout of the Orthodox Jews, paused for their nightly prayers. Nor did Casca hear anywhere the Muslim ritual call to prayer. What he mostly heard were the endless wails of the wounded, the despairing groans of the dying, incessant pleas of: "Water, water. In the name of Allah, give me water."

The adherents of two of the world's great religions were too busy killing and dying to pause to pay their respects to the god for whom they were doing it.

But at last the dying did get their water. The Israeli

water wagons were right behind the ambulances, and men crowded around them gulping from their canteens, refilling them, then gulping them empty to refill them again.

Compassionate Israeli medics moved among the mainly Arab wounded, distributing water as they went.

There never seemed to be enough water, Casca thought, to slake the raging thirst that tore at one's throat as soon as a battle ended.

Not that the battle had, in fact, ended.

CHAPTER ELEVEN

Or even taken pause.

Once inside the outer perimeter of the Egyptian defense, General Tal scattered his armor and men out in the broadest possible line, presenting in the gathering darkness the most difficult of targets for the defending gunners.

The inner defense positions, on the other hand, offered easy and concentrated, if well-protected, targets for the Israeli guns.

Colonel Weintraub set up his H.Q. in one of the Egyptian bunkers, and he held a brief conference of war with his field officers as they wolfed down their food.

The tactic he proposed for his sector of the line was simple enough, and Casca endorsed it readily.

Weintraub divided the defense line into ten sections. He proposed that every possible piece of artillery, howitzers, self-propelled guns, the tank cannons, and every possible captured gun and tank were to be concentrated in turn on each small section of the enemy line.

The concentrated fire coming out of the darkness from dozens of different directions would be very difficult for the Arab gunners to answer. Large sections of the Egyptian line could momentarily be left unattacked as they would be wasting most of their firepower trying to find the widely scattered Israeli guns.

Once the artillery had sufficiently damaged one section and silenced its guns, the big guns could move on to concentrate on another section. In this way, one-tenth of the Egyptian defense would progressively come under attack from all of the Israeli guns.

Then, as one of these sections was silenced, the infantry's heavy weapons squads, recoilless rifles, machine guns, and mortars would move forward to complete the harassment of each section.

And, finally, as always, the PBI, poor bloody infantry, would storm the position, wrest it from its defenders, and eventually turn its firepower on the nearest defense position.

Weintraub asked the ritualistic "Any questions?", got none, and went on. "Let's see if we can raise the Star of David here for sunrise. Move 'em out."

He turned to lead the way out of the bunker and clapped his hand on Casca's shoulder as he passed him.

"Great show, Lonnergan. Your infantry breakthrough was an inspired move. You want to take the first section?"

He didn't wait for an answer, but waved his red helmet to his officers and was gone, sprinting through the darkness to where his armored car waited. The gears grated briefly, the motor roared, and Weintraub was already charging back into battle. His field commanders hastened to catch up with him.

Casca hurried to where his officers and NCOs were eating together and quickly passed on the orders.

Before the last of the light had faded he had seen that the ridge of one great rolling sand dune swept up almost to the enemy walls, and it was here he decided to set up his heavy weapons. He had attached Sergeant Billy Glennon to the heavy weapons squad, which was commanded by an Israeli lieutenant.

There had not been a moment of silence since the first action in the afternoon, but now the noise of the guns reached a deafening crescendo. Hundreds of cannons were trading shells across the small expanse of desert between the inner defenses of Al 'Arish and the perimeter, which was now entirely in Israeli hands. The night sky was lit by the red and orange that belched from gun barrels and exploded from shellbursts.

From one of the captured bunkers Casca directed fire onto his chosen section of the Egyptian defenses. Every Israeli gun joined with him, and the deadly rain poured into the one section of the Arab defense from all over the area.

In a few minutes there were no more flashing muzzles in the selected area, and Casca rushed forward with his heavy weapons squad as the Israeli big guns shifted their attention to the other end of the Egyptian line.

Casca had a clear mental picture of the likely scene in the bunkers beyond the dunes. He knew that the thick concrete and heavy steel would be mainly undamaged, but it was also clear, as the defenders had ceased firing, that the bombardment had penetrated the walls in a number of places. And he also knew, from bitter personal experience, that once high-explosive shells did succeed in penetrating armor, their effect on personnel was heightened as fragments of exploding shells bounced around inside the bunker, ricocheting off the walls and the weaponry, inflicting severe wounds on any human flesh that might be encountered, while the confinement amplified the enormous noise and concussive effect, bursting eardrums and bulging eyes from their sockets.

It was not hard to guess why these Egyptian guns were

no longer firing. But it was now Casca's task to ensure that they did not fire again.

Inside the bunker a few brave souls were, no doubt, lurching amongst the debris, sweating and swearing as they wrestled overturned guns back into position.

Fire showed through a breach in a bunker wall, and Casca directed all of his machine guns at this light, which betrayed where a section of concrete wall had been broken away.

From the distance he could not tell what he was shooting at, but knew that every round that entered through the hole would have at least some effect on the defenders, and none to their liking. At the very least, it would hamper their efforts to extinguish the fire.

The hole was not large enough to hope for entry with mortar fire, so Casca concentrated the firepower of the Davidkas to the rear of the bunker, again counting on the bunker's own armor to multiply the effects of the mortars' shrapnel, noise, and concussive effect.

He devoted some of his machine guns to spraying the walls of the bunkers to either side of his selected target, hoping to diminish the fire that would otherwise come from those directions.

Even so, one Egyptian machine gun got their range, and, as the tracers started to cut into where they crouched behind the dune, Casca gave the prearranged order.

The heavy weapons stopped firing, their crews flattening into the sand. All the foot soldiers rushed forward in silence, the first men tugging the pins from grenades, nobody firing a shot.

They arrived by the broken bunker wall and hurled several grenades inside, crouching against the bunker wall for protection, hands over their ears as explosion after explosion reverberated within the concrete box.

Atef Lufti, *shotel* in hand, was the first man through the

hole, but he found only poor sport—half a dozen staggering wrecks, clutching at torn abdomens and faces, or with the glazed stare of idiocy, hands clapped in frozen horror over their ears.

Lufti butchered them all anyway.

Casca saw quickly that there was nothing usable in the bunker, but by the time Lufti was through it was quiet, if stinking, and it did at least afford them a breach in the Arab line.

They quickly extinguished the fire, which was dying anyway for lack of fuel.

The Egyptian machine gunners were no longer firing on Billy Glennon's squad as they had disappeared into the blackness of the night the instant they stopped firing. The squad now moved silently up to the bunker and manhandled their machine guns and mortars in through the shell hole. Belatedly the Egyptians realized what was happening and turned their guns on the moving shadows they could just make out in the starlight and the flashes of gunfire. A number of Israelis died, but the weapons were passed through the wall into the bunker.

Farther along the Egyptian defenses the concentrated artillery bombardment had silenced another section of the line, and the barrage was moving on to another site while heavy-weapons squads pinned down the surviving defenders. The rear wall of the bunker opened into a trench that communicated with the other bunkers to either side.

As the first of the alerted Egyptians came running along the trench, Tommy Moynihan opened fire with his Uzi, standing in the open and firing first to one side, then to the other, then leaping back into the bunker as the Arabs opened fire on each other.

The crossfire stopped abruptly, and Moynihan stepped out into the trench once more to spray his Uzi over the confused soldiery to either side.

Both groups of Arabs withdrew, but the respite could only last for seconds.

Over his shoulder Moynihan glanced back into the bunker. "Go man," Casca shouted, "I'll take this side."

Before the Arabs could regroup, both their bunkers were under attack from the rear. And a couple of grenades quickly solved what was left of the problem. Casca now held all three bunkers and their communication trench.

But, he reasoned, it would quickly become too hot to hold. Then he thought, By the teeth of Mars, I could use a few seconds to think. Nothing for it but to keep going. They clambered out of the trench onto the sands behind the bunker and paused in a dune trough about fifty yards away.

Billy Glennon had the machine gun ready just as the first mortar shells landed in the trench they had just quit, but Casca's hand restrained Billy's from the trigger.

Casca did a rough count of the silent, crouching figures. About half his company had made it this far. Not too bad. He knew some were still out with the heavy weapons behind the dune from where they had launched this attack.

From one of the bunkers bursts of submachine gunfire greeted the Arabs who followed their mortar shells into the trench, and Casca realized that he still had a few men in the bunkers. They had better come out pretty soon or they would be cut off by much larger Arab numbers.

Well, perhaps he had only lost about a quarter of his company. So be it. The ways of war. They couldn't be changed. Not by Casca. Not by Mars himself.

But if they all didn't move pretty soon, they would be cut off. Beyond the farther rise of the dune there was a large, square building, probably a store of some sort. He pointed it out to Billy and the big Paddy hefted his machine gun around and sprayed it liberally with lead.

To their astonishment there was no answer, but they

were already rushing for it anyway, Uzis blazing from
their hips. Casca saw a door and threw himself at it
shoulder-first. Wood splintered, a lock tore loose, and he
tumbled inside. His Kalashnikov came up ready to fire,
but there was no need to shoot. Or rather, there was great
need not to shoot. Casca pointed the muzzle of his rifle to
the floor, and motioned similarly to the others who were
rushing through the door after him.

There was just enough light to see the racks of weapons
and the crates of ammunition.

"Oh shit," Casca groaned, "what a target we make
here."

Billy Glennon arrived, bringing up the rear, toting the
heavy Browning like a toy. "Well," he said with a chuckle,
"we'll have something to hold it with anyway. I've got a
dreadful dislike for running out of ammunition."

The rest of the company was now crowding into the
building. Billy Glennon opened a timber window flap and
hastened to set up his machine gun to cover the direction
they had come from. On the other side of the room Harry
Russell was doing the same, and at the other walls soldiers
were carefully easing open the wooden shutters.

They found that they enjoyed a clear field of fire in
every direction. They were in possession, and, so far, they
were not under attack.

"Could be a lot worse," Moynihan grunted, opening
his canteen and swallowing thirstily.

Casca opened his canteen and swallowed too. Then a
thought struck him as he saw others doing the same.

"Hey, we'd better take it easy on the water. It might be
a while before we see that water wagon."

All around the room men reluctantly screwed the caps
on their canteens as they realized that the battle was far
from over, and a long way from won. Their eyes flickered

about the room, but the only liquid in sight was in some fire extinguishers on the walls.

Casca promptly lost interest in the water situation. If they should get pinned down inside this cache of high explosive, all the water in the Aswan High Dam wouldn't save them. He knew well enough the raging thirst that follows every battle. His concerns were now outside thirst. The numberless campaigns that he had endured had forced him to think like a dispassionate general, regardless of how his tongue might be frying, or his wounds hurting.

He had learned in the hardest possible way how to ignore, or at worst suppress, the demands of his body so that he could keep that body alive through whatever demands battle might make upon it.

Doomed as he was to an eternity of soldiering, he had come to hate and fear death. He could confront it when necessary, as he had as a boy soldier in Caesar's legions, but the curse of Christ had deprived him of the luxury of welcoming his death in the very moment of that confrontation. For every death that he suffered now had to be endured over again as the endless curse took effect and his body agonizingly reknitted so that he might live again—to die again.

Not dying had become a very high priority, and each time he succeeded in not dying he got better at avoiding death. His present situation, however, was making him wonder if two thousand years of soldiering had taught him anything after all.

The main thrust of the battle, as planned, had moved away from the sector that he had first brought under attack. And now he was in possession of a powder keg.

To be sure, the position was secure for the moment, the field of fire open, the scope for enemy counterattack limited. But it might take only one tracer bullet, or a single grenade—not to mention a rocket—to blow the whole shebang into eternity.

An idea came to Casca. He tried to push it away, but it persisted, so he entertained it and explored its possibilities.

Very well, he thought, here he was, right back where it had all started 1,935 years earlier. Long enough time surely. Maybe by now he was within reach of release. The Jew had cursed him to wait for his return, so there was the implicit promise that the curse would not last forever. The dying revolutionary had not said when or how or why he would return, but a thousand other prophets had chanced their arm on the point. And most of them, almost all of them, made it about now. But from their words, it had looked like about now for most of the nineteen hundred years that Casca had waited for his release.

Yet this time there was one big difference. He was back in the land where the curse had first been laid upon him.

The poet that lurks unrealized in every man cried out in Casca for a final resolution of his eternal dilemma in the place where it had been born.

And now, perhaps in a way that he could have never thought of, the resolution might be in sight.

If, as seemed likely, one round from the Arabs were to arrive within this building stacked to the ceiling with high explosive, then surely he would die.

Surely, he would *really* die.

How could even the curse of the vengeance-minded crucified one put back together a body so blown apart? The flesh wound in his side had already healed, but that had been a mere scratch.

Casca had a horrifying but also liberating vision of being blown apart, blasted to the four winds by any chance round that might arrive. And, surely, that must be the end.

Across the top of a pile of rockets his eyes connected with Hyman Hagkel's.

"The End of Days, do you think?" Hymie smiled at him, his fanatical eyes clearly lusting toward his own death.

In Casca's soul a tiny dissonance trembled. He shook his head.

"Just one more end to one more day," he said. "And it's up to us how it ends. Let's get to it."

With sudden determined resolution he moved to where Billy Glennon's Browning commanded the field of their most likely source of attack.

"See anything?" he asked.

"Damnedest field of fire I've ever looked over," Glennon grunted without taking his eyes from the area covered by his gun. "Where the hell are they? If they don't want to fight, why don't they just lie down and die?"

Throughout the area that was exactly what the Egyptians were doing. Some of them were simply collapsing behind their guns, paralyzed with fright; some were hiding; some were running. But almost none were fighting.

The officer-led Israeli Army had found for its enemy an officerless rabble of young boys and tired old professionals.

And none of the boys, and few of the pros, had ever experienced a battle like this one. They were reeling in horror and despair from scenes of spurting blood and spilled guts that were all the more terrifying because they happened in the dark. And the bits and pieces of dismembered bodies flying around alerted the Arabs to their own imminent fate.

As dawn broke over the Sinai there was not a single Egyptian officer in effective command in the whole of Al 'Arish, although here and there a captain or a major, a colonel or a sergeant tried to rally around him a few Arabs in the defense of their Jihad.

A few succeeded, but these heroes died as painfully, as

brutally, and as uselessly as the cowards and the sensible ones who were running for the horizon.

Casca's company played little further part in the action. The arms store was a fine place to rest but no sort of bunker to fight from. And, hell, the company had lost enough men for one day. The Egyptians were either unaware that they had occupied the building or were too busy running, hiding, and dying to care.

Only when the Arab defense positions emptied in a wholesale, every-man-for-himself retreat, did Casca permit his troops to open fire. They sprayed the few Arabs who came close with lead, but attracted no return fire amid the general chaos. As the sun came up Casca was delighted to realize that his ammunition store had survived intact and that the fleeing Arabs were making no attempt upon it.

Over the Regimental Headquarters a large blue-and-white flag was rippling in the light morning breeze.

"Well, you learn all the time," he said with a laugh to Harry Russell. "The last place I'd have ever wanted to be in turns out to be the safest position there is."

Harry sat down on an ammunition case.

"Yeah," he said, "it sure is an unusual sort of bunker—but I like it."

CHAPTER TWELVE

Brigadier General Israel Tal invited his field officers to a working breakfast in the luxuriously appointed Egyptian general officers' dining room.

"Fruits of victory," he said ironically as he passed around a plate of fresh figs. "A brutal battle, but we have set the stage, as we planned to, for the victories that are to follow.

"I have just been advised that an Egyptian relief column is on the way here consisting of an armored brigade and a brigade of mechanized infantry." He paused for effect. "I must also tell you that we will not be waiting for them as they will not get here. They had the misfortune to encounter Avraham Yoffe's men at Bîr al Lahtan." He grinned happily as his officers cheered. "So we will be pushing on immediately—to Suez."

There was another general cheer. "Some of us, that is. Some of you I am sending to the assistance of General Sharon, who is about to attack Abu Agheila. He is at present encircling the whole area, which is, as you know, an extremely complex maze of fortifications that has been built up over many years, and will not be easy to take.

"But we must have it. It commands the central axis through the Sinai. Ariel Sharon will launch a coordinated attack of infantry and armor at nightfall today. Colonel Weintraub's regiment will join him. The force will be lifted from here by helicopter."

"Sounds like a fun way to start the night," Moynihan said when Casca told him the news. "I suppose they'll put us down right in the middle of it all."

Moynihan had guessed right. The helicopters swooped into the center of a ring of fire.

General Sharon's concerted attack was occupying the Egyptians at every point of the compass. For an hour every gun that he could bring to bear had been firing as hard and as fast as the barrels could stand.

Shells were landing all along the perimeter of the fortress's outer defenses while other guns were pouring more and more shells into every corner of the inner perimeter. The Israeli Air Force had spent the last two hours of daylight plastering the entire area.

The attacking bombers and strafing fighters had the sky to themselves as there was not an Egyptian plane left in condition to fly.

Wave after wave of Vautour bombers pounded the fortifications. The Arab antiaircraft gunners tried valiantly to make up for their lack of air defense, but only succeeded in exposing themselves as targets for the escorting fighter planes. By the time Colonel Weintraub's helicopters arrived there was scarcely a gun crew left that could fire into the air.

The timing was meticulous. The incessant bombardment cloaked the arrival of the airborne force and ceased only half a minute before the first choppers set down and troops leaped from them.

The dazed, bewildered, and thoroughly scared defenders barely registered that the helicopters were coming. Their attention was entirely devoted to the desperate effort of trying to answer the encircling artillery barrage.

Casca deployed his men in a protective circle around his heavy-weapons squad and succeeded in keeping at bay the few Egyptian troops who attempted to attack them.

Then the mortars and the Brownings opened up and the startled defenders discovered that their front was behind them. After hours of heartbreaking, suicidal effort to organize their fire onto the attackers out in the desert, they now had to try to regroup to fight into the center of their own area.

And they had barely managed to start thinking about that when General Sharon's armor and infantry came swarming at them from all over the desert.

The battle was over almost as soon as it had begun. Sandwiched in the dark between the paratroopers and the encircling force, the Egyptians scarcely knew which way to turn. When they fired, they frequently hit their own troops. When they thought about running, they ran into some sort of fire, no matter which way they ran.

It was a situation that would easily enough bring brave men to tears—and most of these defenders were mere schoolboys. Last night they had dreamed of glory, medals, admiring women, envious men. Tonight this nightmare was real beyond all dreaming.

Terrified, they broke out of their own defenses to run directly into Sharon's machine guns.

The carnage continued.

And ended only when the Israelis tired of the slaughter. Gradually, first in one section of the circle, then in others, Israeli soldiers stopped shooting. The despairing Arab survivors rushed out as the Israelis walked in, their guns held loose in their hands, or even slung over their shoulders.

Section after section quieted until there was only sporadic fire here and there.

And then silence, except for the panic-stricken shouts of the thousands of Arabs who were running heedlessly into the dark, the screams of the wounded, and the hideous groans of the dying.

The battle was over.

"An unjoyous victory," Billy Glennon muttered as he recapped his canteen. "I haven't even raised a thirst."

"No," Moynihan said, grimacing, "me neither. But I'll bet ye these boyohs who are heading away could use a drop."

"Yeah," Glennon agreed. He well knew the truly unquenchable thirst that followed defeat in a firefight. "Dunno where they'll find any."

"Well," Moynihan said, "Screw 'em, they picked the wrong side."

"Born into it," Harry Russell said, "but we seem to be on the right side this time."

"I wish you hadn't said that."

"So do I. Damn my big mouth, so do I."

CHAPTER THIRTEEN

Part of General Tal's task force racing west from Al 'Arish had already made it to the Suez Canal.

The helicopters returned to Abu Agheila and the Red colonel's regiment was ferried out—but not back to rejoin General Tal. They were delivered to Jerusalem, where fierce fighting was raging as possession of the ancient city was contested by Israeli and Jordanian troops.

In the 1956 war, King Hussein had kept his troops aloof from the action, and it had been Israel's hope that he would do the same now, but Jordanian forces had opened fire on the Israeli part of Jerusalem within twenty-five minutes of the Israeli sneak attacks on Egyptian airfields that had signaled the start of the war.

Minister for Defense Moshe Dayan, hoping for a Jordanian withdrawal, had withheld permission to retaliate until one o'clock that afternoon. Even then he gave the Israeli commander, General Uvi Narkiss, strict orders to ensure that on no account should any damage occur to any of the holy places sacred to either Jews, Moslems, or Christians.

All day and all night Monday and Tuesday the battle had continued. Israeli troops had captured the headquarters

of the UN truce force and had advanced through the
Mandelbaum Gate to fight a fierce battle for the Police
School. The British-trained Arab Legion put up a stubborn
and almost successful defense. Throughout Monday and
Tuesday nights the Jewish quarter of the city was subjected
to heavy artillery bombardment. There were almost a thou-
sand casualties amongst the Jewish civilian population.
Now, in a series of flanking movements, the Israelis had
taken the high ground around Jerusalem, sealing off the
Old City, but leaving an escape route into Jordan for the
Arab defenders.

Casca's company was landed on the Mount of Olives to
the east of the city above the Garden of Gethsemane.
Israeli artillery was firing slowly and intermittently into the
city, the coordinates for each shot being carefully studied
before the commanding officer would give the order to
fire. Major Epstein was trying to clear the Jordanians from
the area inside St. Stephen's Gate on the northeastern
corner of the city. But he had to ensure that none of his
shells landed on the Christian Church of St. Anne or the
nearby Dome of the Rock. He was doing a sterling job of
it, but as a result the Jordanians were not being dislodged.
They had ensconced themselves beyond the western wall
of the Church of St. Anne, between Herod's Gate and the
sacred site of the Antonia Fortress.

Casca watched the artillery officer poring over his maps,
checking and rechecking his coordinates.

"Oh, wouldn't I just love to land a shell on that damn
dome," Epstein said with a scowl.

"Fire away," Casca said. "History has forgiven Napo-
leon for destroying the Parthenon, and it was a much
grander temple than the Dome of the Rock."

"History is apt to be kinder than Moshe Dayan. Like
myself, he doesn't even go to synagogue, but he has

forbidden me to so much as put a scratch on any sacred site."

Casca laughed. "Every corner of this city is sacred to somebody."

"You said it," Epstein moaned, "and Dayan has made them all sacred to me. And I'm a died-in-the-wool atheist."

"You're not a Sabra, are you?"

"Hell no, I'm Dutch. I'm just an Arab hater on principle."

"What principle is that?"

Epstein laughed easily. "Who knows? Everybody needs somebody to hate. I hate Arabs." He thought for a moment. "You know, I suspect it's because they are really Semites, and I really am not."

It was Casca's turn to laugh. "Now you're getting me confused."

"Anybody who is not confused about Arabs and Jews simply has no idea of what is what," Epstein answered. "As far as I can tell, my problem dates back to medieval Russia when, on the advice of his scholars, the czar ordered his subjects to embrace the Jewish religion. They resisted mightily, and the czar invented the pogrom, massacring and torturing for a generation until a number of areas did, in fact, convert to Judaism.

"Then the czar changed his mind, declared Judaism an illegal religion, and applied his pogroms to trying to wipe it out."

"And these new Jews resisted?" Casca asked.

"Strenuously," Epstein replied. "Even more strenuously than their parents had resisted conversion. They had been cowed once and could not accept it a second time. Besides, by this time they believed themselves to be the chosen people—something not easy to give up.

"So the pogroms and persecutions continued as they do

to this day. Somewhere along the way my people fled to Poland, a few generations later to Germany, and eventually to Holland.

"And eventually, I fled here so that I can feel persecuted. In Holland we are no longer sufficiently ill treated for me to feel like a real Jew. Understand?"

"No." Casca laughed.

"Nor do I." Epstein laughed too.

"And the Arabs?" Casca asked.

"Well, meanwhile, a madman, somewhat in the style of Christ, but more violent—his name is now Mohammed— was busy here running a pogrom of his own, putting to the sword every Jew who would not bow down to Allah.

"So, at the point of the Muslim sword, most of the Jews who had stayed here after the fall of Jerusalem became Muslims. A few, the Sephardic, held out and fled to Abyssinia. Today they scarcely even speak Hebrew. They're called Falasha.

"So now, we Jews of Russian race, the Ashkenazis, but of Jewish religion, are fighting a Semitic race that is Muslim by religion. Moses, Christ, and Mohammed would all be confused if they were to come here today."

"And how," asked Casca, "will it end, do you think?"

"It will never end." Epstein shrugged and returned his attention to his maps.

The Red colonel trundled his armored car up to the wall near where the Arabs waited in safety by St. Stephen's Gate on the edge of the Muslim Quarter. Weintraub called up a Centurion tank and waved it on past him and into the wall. As the masonry crumbled Weintraub followed the Centurion through the broken wall, and Casca and his company rushed behind his armored car.

They came under heavy fire from all around the Church of St. Anne and were forced to take shelter behind the armor, trading rifle shots with the Jordanians.

Every burst of fire brought several in reply from the well-placed Arabs. Casualties mounted rapidly on both sides as the tedious firefight continued under the ever hotter sun.

Moynihan led his squad in a blistering charge that dislodged Arabs from a large house, but then they were pinned down by Arab fire from several quarters.

Harry Russell led another charge that took the adjoining house and then Casca, Billy Glennon, and a whole platoon managed to leap-frog these positions and occupy the old inn on the corner of the street that led to the Damascus Gate.

Moynihan and Russell brought up their squads and as the rest of the troops moved up, they had command of several blocks of the Muslim Quarter.

"Just like fighting the cops in Belfast," Moynihan muttered as he charged back into the street again.

At the end of an hour they were halfway to the Damascus Gate. But the Jordanian troops rallied strongly and mounted a series of furious charges along the narrow, twisting streets that surrounded Casca's men.

"B'Jazus, but these Johnnies can fight," Harry Russell cursed as he fired around a stone wall, covering his men as they fell back toward the old inn.

He was limping painfully when he made it back to the inn. An Arab bullet had singed his buttock as he had turned to run after his men.

"It's a right mournful thing for an Irishman to get shot in the ass," he groaned. "It's bad enough to have to run, but to bear the mark of it is a bitter pill."

"Better than being shot in the balls," Moynihan said.

"There is that about it," Russell agreed, then scowled and cursed as Casca poured alcohol over the graze.

He twisted his neck to try to see the undignified wound.

"It's a sorrowful place to be hit for certain," he lamented. "Can't be bandaged, I can't sit down—and it's ruined me best Sunday trousers."

"We'll get you a smart new pair made by the best Jewish tailor as soon as we're through here," said Moynihan. "Which might be a wee while," he went on, peeking around a window shutter at a street entirely held by Jordanians. "I think they've got us holed up here."

Russell was gulping water from his canteen. "Have you ever noticed how your thirst increases when you're taking a licking?"

"Aye," Moynihan said, drinking, too, as they all were. "Don't know if there's any decent water here."

"Bound to be some wine," Russell said.

"I suppose so, but that's not what I need."

"I'll just have a look," Harry Russell said and headed toward the steps that led down to the cellars.

Moynihan looked after him with a puzzled frown. When it came to drinking Harry was no slouch, but only a novice alongside Moynihan. But neither of them ever drank on the job.

Russell reappeared with a bottle in each hand. He craned his neck around the shutter and withdrew it smartly as a shot ricocheted from the wall. "Aye, we're going to be here a wee while."

He ran his bayonet up the sloping neck of the bottle and beamed as it popped off the top inch of glass and the cork. He held the neatly broken neck just away from his lips and gulped several mouthfuls.

Moynihan shook his head as Harry offered him the bottle. So did Casca and the others. Russell shrugged and drank some more. "I'd enjoy this more if I could sit down to it." He laughed.

He drained the bottle and, using the same technique to

open it, started on the second. Moynihan glanced at him and shrugged. Well, two bottles of light table wine was no big deal for a drinker like Harry, especially with the battle thirst on him.

Casca was thinking along the same lines. His old comrade's behavior had him slightly puzzled, but his mind and his eyes were mainly on the street.

House-to-house fighting was his element. He had survived more street confrontations than any hundred men alive—if only because he had also died in a dozen or more inner-city battles. But this city was something else.

And he knew this city.

In this very inn, nineteen hundred-odd years earlier, he had stabbed to death his own sergeant. And had died for it. And lived again.

Over the intervening centuries, the inn had been ruined and rebuilt a dozen, perhaps a hundred times. The room where he and the sergeant had fought over the whore now lay beneath his feet, under the accumulated debris of the ages. The cellar from which Harry had looted the wine was built way above the roof of the inn where that fight had taken place.

The Damascus Gate was still where it had been then. So was Herod's Gate, and several other landmarks. But the territory between had changed beyond all recognition. Where there had once been hollows there were now hills, built up by the endless rebuilding of the city upon its own ruins. And the great landmarks, the Dome of the Rock, the Church of the Holy Sepulcher, the Citadel, and the Tower of David, which had all once stood proud upon heights, were now sunk in the hollows between the giant mounds of the repeated reconstruction.

And in between, the streets were a mad, meaningless maze that twisted and turned in every conceivable direc-

tion, a warren of cobbled alleys winding through arches
over and around the mounds of the ruins below. Streets
that had once run level now climbed in flights of steps or
descended in steep ramps, or simply came to an abrupt end
in blunt walls.

And the Jordanians they were fighting had lived here for
generations. They knew this territory, and they knew how
to fight.

It came down to the old dilemma. When all strategy
fails there are just two choices: run or attack.

And there was nowhere for the Israelis to run.

"We're going to move out," Casca said.

"About time, I reckon," Harry Russell said. He pointed
west down the one straight street, the Via Dolorosa. "Okay
if I take my squad right down there?"

Casca had been thinking of leading that charge himself.
"I think that will be pretty rough."

The big Paddy smiled and Casca caught a whiff of the
wine on his breath as he spoke. "If ye've got a better idea,
I'm here to take orders."

Casca nodded. "Okay, Harry, it's yours. Move out."

They poured out of the inn a dozen different ways,
through doors and windows, over courtyard walls, up into
the middle of the street from an old storm drain. The
sudden fury of their charge set the Arabs reeling.

Casca and Moynihan and their men made it to the
Damascus Gate and forced its defenders from the towers.

Now they had command of another straight street, the
el-Wad Road, a major north-south artery that intersected
the Via Dolorosa. From atop the gate Casca could see
Harry's men fighting their way along the Dolorosa one
house at a time. When they occupied a house on one side
of the street, they would use its windows and roof to lay a
withering hail of fire on the house opposite. Then a sudden

pause and a mad charge directly across the street to storm the enemy-held building.

Then this new vantage point would enable them to pour similar fire on the next house opposite. Casca noticed that Harry was limping much worse, and guessed that he had been hit again.

The loss of the Damascas Gate had sapped the morale of the Jordanians in the el-Wad Road, and coming under Billy Glennon's fire from their own machine guns demoralized them completely. In a few more minutes Moynihan was greeting Harry Russell where the street met the Via Dolorosa. The greeting died in his throat.

Harry was standing erect, but only because one long arm above his head supported him on the wall. Moynihan watched in horror as the Uzi dropped from his other arm. There were several red holes in the chest of his uniform. Blood poured from his mouth as he opened it to smile. Moynihan reached him as he crashed to the cobblestones.

"Last fight, Tommy lad." He grinned up at him.

Moynihan struggled for a moment to answer. "Nonsense. There'll be lots more fights, you gossoon."

"Not for me old omithorn," Casca arrived to hear him say. "There's a last fight for all of us." As Harry died, Casca sighed that it could not be so for him. Through the sounds of gunfire he could hear Tommy grind his teeth.

The little Irishman dropped the empty magazine from his Uzi and deliberately clipped another in its place.

"Which way to the Wailing Wall?" he gritted to Casca.

Casca pointed south along the el-Wad Road.

Moynihan stepped out to the center of the roadway and walked slowly south. His squad fanned out and accompanied him along the sidewalks.

A burst of submachine-gun fire kicked up dust ahead of him. Moynihan pointed his Uzi at the Arabs on a balcony.

He squeezed off a single shot, which missed, but the Jordanians were almost cut in two by the concentrated fire on half a dozen of Moynihan's men.

He walked on unhurriedly, drawing fire now and then from the occasional Jordanian who had stayed under cover to rearguard their general withdrawal.

Tommy's deliberate marksmanship accounted for some of them. The concentrated firepower of his men took care of the rest. After an hour Israeli troops held most of the Muslim Quarter, including the Dome of the Rock and the Mosque of al-Aqsa.

Casca ran to the mosque. At the entrance he carefully carried out the ritual prescribed for a devout Muslim. The faithful had fled into the interior, but one old priest watched in amazement as this man in the uniform of the army of the Jews went meticulously through the ritual of the faithful.

Casca made his way into the mosque proper. His only transgression was the Kalashnikov slung over his shoulder. He couldn't tell whether it was the rifle or his devout manner that kept the Arabs at a respectful distance.

He headed for the carved wooden pulpit and paused before it. "Not bad," he whispered to himself as if he were praying quietly. "Still here after all this time."

The last time he had been inside this mosque was as one of Saladin's hosts on October 9, 1187. Saladin had paced the pulpit as he prayed after capturing Jerusalem from the Crusaders.

He made a last small obeisance and ran back into the street. By noon, fighting street by street, house by house, room by room, the Israeli troops had broken through to what had once been the Jewish Quarter, but where no Jew had been allowed to live since Jordan gained control of the city in 1948. They headed for the Dung Gate that led out of the Old City on the edge of the steep slopes that led down to the Valley of Kidron. The slopes were clear of Jordanians and they returned their attention to within the city walls.

An hour later they were fighting in the Christian Quarter and in the Armenian Quarter, and by fourteen hundred hours the Israelis were in possession of New Gate, the Tower of David, and the Zion Gate. The whole of the Old City was under Israeli control.

At the wheel of a jeep, Major General Moshe Dayan drove through the Mandelbaum Gate to the Wailing Wall, all that was left of the Second Temple. He walked to the Wall and placed a prayer in a chink between its stones.

"Damn near two thousand years since a yid last did that," Hymie said.

"D'ye ken what it says?" Moynihan nudged Hymie.

"Let peace reign in Israel," the New Yorker answered.

"Only in Israel?" wondered Moynihan. "Well, at least he hasn't asked that we be put out of business altogether."

"And he's not likely to." Hymie laughed. "We're getting very big in the arms business."

Tommy lifted his head to look around the city square crammed with stretchers carrying Israelis and Jordanians swathed in bloodstained bandages. He looked down at where Harry Russell's long frame overspanned his stretcher. "I'm starting to think that I could use a change."

"Me too," said Casca. "Next time I go to war I might try a navy."

The whole perimeter of the city was now in Israeli hands, but there were Arab diehards holding out on rooftops, in cellars and basements, in the abundant secret courtyards, and in disused drains.

For Casca, mopping up was the most distasteful phase of an inner-city battle. The task was profoundly boring, but infinitely dangerous. Every house, every room, every cupboard had to be searched.

Inevitably one's attention flagged. After looking into a thousand closets, somebody would eventually open one carelessly.

And that would be the one that concealed a die-hard fanatic with a handful of primed grenades.

Or maybe the door would tug on a trip-wire that would detonate a cache of explosives that would bring the whole house down.

There were other ugly experiences too. A stirring in a dark corner would be greeted with a quick burst of submachine-gun fire—and a tiny girl shielding a baby brother in her arms would tumble dying from their hiding place.

Demented elderly people would be found standing in the center of empty rooms from which everybody, including their reason, had fled.

One always stumbled upon wounded who were beyond help, orphaned children, bereaved parents.

Mopping up was an operation that Casca would have loved to delegate to others, but he knew that it was a phase of war where experience counted most—and he had the most experience.

Several of the houses had small, shallow holes scratched into the stone by the front door. They had once held a mezuzah, the small case that contained a piece of parchment inscribed with two passages from Deuteronomy.

Casca came upon one of these on the third story of an Arab household. The lower two floors were occupied by a large Arab family. Yet the mezuzah was intact in its small stone cache.

An elderly Arab had followed him up the stairs and he now bowed, introduced himself as Abu Lachim, and handed him a key.

"Booby trap," Casca's mind shouted to him.

He searched the old Arab's eyes. Their flat, brown opaqueness told him nothing. But they were not the eyes of a fanatic.

He motioned to his men to return downstairs. An Israeli sergeant stayed by the head of the staircase.

Gingerly Casca turned the key, then the doorknob, and lastly he booted open the door.

Nothing happened.

Casca waited a moment while his eyes became accustomed to the gloom, then stepped carefully into the dark room. After another moment's pause he crossed to the windows and threw open the shutters.

The light fell on a gold-lettered sign written in Hebrew that proclaimed the large room as the Torat Hayim Synagogue. On a gold bookstand the Torah stood open. The prie-dieus and study tables were clean and polished. Around the edges of the huge room were thousands of carefully stacked books. On a large table in the center of the room a number of books were lying open in front of chairs.

Casca saw that these books were all in Hebrew. He turned to the Arab. "A Jewish congregation prays here?"

"Oh no." Abu's wrinkled face broke into a smile. "Nobody except my family has entered this room since the Jews left this area."

"When Jordan occupied the city?"

"Of course. The congregation of this synagogue fled." He gestured at the open books. "As you can see, they left in a hurry."

"So how does it happen that it's all still here, undisturbed?"

Abu looked at him, not quite comprehending the question.

"Nobody has come to disturb."

"But it all looks . . . cared for."

The old Arab shrugged. "My family stacked the books.

We sweep the floor, dust once in a while.'' He added defensively, ''It is a room in our house.''

''But it's a Jewish synagogue. You maintain a prayer-house of infidels?''

''Why not?'' Abu shrugged again. ''In this room the Jews prayed to God. There is no God but God.''

The Israeli sergeant clapped the old man on the back. ''Abu, with your wisdom we could have avoided the whole of this damned war between our people.''

''Except for the oil,'' Casca muttered under his breath.

CHAPTER FOURTEEN

Weintraub became the Red General, and Casca was promoted again, this time to lieutenant colonel, and given command of a regiment.

With the city of Jerusalem secured, Weintraub's force was divided. Casca's regiment was sent south to attack Bethlehem, while another force moved north on Ramallah, the site of Radio Jordan. A third force moved east to attack Jericho.

Casca's force arrived on the outskirts of Bethlehem in the late afternoon and he lost no time in pressing his attack. Casca led the assault, as all Israeli officers were expected to, in his armored car, Billy Glennon at the wheel, racing for the Jordanian defenses in the first wave of assault vehicles.

They immediately came under heavy fire from the entrenched Arabs, but the defending gunners accomplished little. Casca had left all of his infantry and most of his armor in reserve, feinting with only the lightest and fastest vehicles.

Naturally, the first of the Arab artillery fire fell short, but the pattern of shell bursts moved rapidly closer to the broad, advancing front of Israeli armor.

Then the shells were bursting right in front of them.

"Faster, faster," Casca bellowed, and Glennon changed gears and tramped on the gas pedal for an extra burst of acceleration.

All the other drivers followed suit in Casca's prearranged maneuver, and the Arab gunners suddenly found that their shells were now falling to the rear of the attacking force. At Casca's orders no Israeli guns had yet spoken. Now Epstein fired the cannon that he had been carefully sighting and resighting all through the charge.

He scored a direct hit with his third shot, and all along the line other gunners had similar successes. The stationary guns in Casca's reserve had an even greater devastating effect as they had had plenty of time to locate and aim for the Arab guns, all of which had been provoked into revealing themselves.

Now the Jordanians were frantically cranking down the elevation of their guns and the pattern of shell bursts came uncomfortably close.

"Stop!" Casca shouted, and Billy Glennon and then the other drivers stood on their brakes.

In a great, swirling cloud of dust the entire force came to a halt, then turned to race back toward where the reserve force waited.

The confused Arab gunners now had to readjust their aim once more. A few lucky shots scored hits, but most of Casca's vehicles made the turn unscathed, the APCs unloading their cargo of sappers and their equipment before they hurried after the rest of the retiring armor.

Meanwhile Casca's stationary guns were firing at will, scoring direct hit after direct hit on the Arab guns. The rest of Casca's armor and the infantry now rolled forward while his artillery laid down an increasingly accurate barrage on the defenders' guns. Casca's small attack force retired through his own lines to rest and refuel.

Casca joined Major Epstein in directing the artillery and together they watched the effect of their bombardment as it accounted for gun after gun in the defending positions. The sappers had now succeeded in clearing a narrow track through the mines and at their signal some empty APCs raced forward of the main force to gather them up as the first squadron of tanks changed direction for the gap in the minefield.

From behind the second line of Bethlehem's defenses a squadron of huge Stalin tanks appeared, intent on challenging the Israeli tanks on the open ground beyond the mined area.

The artillery major acted quickly and a number of Casca's guns that had not yet been used opened fire on the tanks. The gunners had fired only a few rounds since the beginning of the battle, just enough to sight in their weapons on the range to the major Arab defense line. Now they needed only a few more rounds to bring their big guns to bear where the tanks were coming from behind the line.

The Stalins and a huge force of infantry were advancing in three lines, obviously moving along a clear track through a minefield. The major marked his military map as he called coordinates to his gunners, concentrating their fire in the vicinity of the lead tanks. He shouted lustily as the first hit was scored and marked the spot as near as he could guess on his map.

From behind the crippled Stalin two other tanks were trying to push it clear. Epstein joyfully hammered a rain of shells onto the three tanks.

But the Arabs succeeded in pushing the crippled tank clear and the column was moving forward again. The Israeli gunners, however, now had the area zeroed in and they unleashed a hail of fire that crippled the entire column. A number of Stalins tried to maneuver out of the line to escape the furious barrage, but only succeeded in running onto their own mines.

Casca raced for his armored car and in another minute was racing for the wrecked tanks, the whole of his light-armor squadron tearing along behind him.

From up ahead the Red general's car was also heading for the scene of the carnage. He had with him a number of heavy Centurions, and as the artillery barrage ceased these quickly got into position to push the ruined Stalins aside.

APCs and jeeps were spilling Israeli infantry onto the sand in the now clearly defined mine-safe area. They opened up on the dazed Jordanian infantry who, still reeling from the bombardment, could not regroup to answer the fire. They broke and ran, those on the outer edges of the mob being blown skywards in pieces as they set off antipersonnel mines.

Soon there was something like a straight line of fleeing Jordanians running for the protection of their fortress. They jostled each other as they ran, all trying to stay toward the center of the path through the minefield.

Behind them came the armor of Casca and the Red general as well as a number of APCs and Bren gun carriers, their crews pouring lead at the backs of the retreating horde.

Then they were through the Jordanian lines and the Israeli armor was fanning out to either side and wrecking increasing devastation as more and more vehicles and men poured through the breach.

In another hour the battle was over. The Star of David was flying over yet another Arab fortress.

The Israeli high command ordered Casca to secure the city and ensure that it could be held against a Jordanian counterattack.

A quick count revealed that they had captured roughly fifty tanks, dozens of field guns, scores of trucks and jeeps, thousands of gallons of gasoline and diesel fuel, enormous numbers of weapons of every type, and whole storerooms of ammunition.

The city of Bethlehem also had an adequate storage of potable water and plenty of food. Ninety percent of the city's defenses were still intact, and Casca was quickly convinced that he could hold the city against any force that Jordan was likely to send to the attack.

He gave half his troops six hours' leave, and his jeep was amongst the first to leave the barracks. Billy Glennon was at the wheel and Major Epstein and Hymie in the back. Not far behind came another Jeep carrying Moynihan, Wardi Nathan, Atef Lufti, and David Levy.

They stopped at an Arab sidewalk café where the owner had just taken down the shutters. He came toward them apprehensively, bowing deeply from a little distance.

"Terrified for his life, but as eager to rob us as ever," sneered Epstein. "Give us some wine, you Arab dog," he shouted, and the Arab scuttled speedily away.

Even the abrupt Moynihan looked askance at the uncalled-for rudeness. Casca's eyes met Billy's and they both smiled. Hell, so they hated each other, it was their war.

The tables quickly filled with Israeli officers and men, colonels, sergeants, and privates sitting together easily. It was part of the Israeli Army egalitarian tradition and also grew out of the citizen-soldier nature of this army. A sergeant heading for another table slapped Major Epstein on the back as he passed and Epstein playfully stuck out a leg to trip him. A week earlier Epstein had been maintenance manager in a small factory. The sergeant owned the factory.

Moynihan approved of the wine and ordered more. He was not quite as rude as Epstein, but followed to the letter the Israeli Army briefing on how to deal with the defeated enemy. He was arrogant, overbearing, acted as if the restaurateur were determined to rob him, sell him watered or maybe poisoned wine, or stab him in the back if he got half a chance.

The Arab accepted this treatment as the defeated learn to do anywhere, and was grateful that it was not worse. Amongst Arabs the legend from World War II still survived of the Australian Ninth Division who, after a defeat of Rommel, staged such an orgy of rapacious looting that Goebbels dubbed them the Forty Thousand Thieves.

Moynihan and Glennon were not in the mood for drinking. They only drank a couple glasses of wine each. Six hours was nowhere near enough to do the job properly, and they scorned to do a job half well. In fact, they knew that there was every chance they might be in action again by morning and a battle was no place to take a hangover. And a battle in the desert was no place for a raging thirst.

They left the café and wandered the streets on foot in twos and threes. Whores beckoned to them from balconies and windows, and soon Casca and Epstein were walking alone. Epstein's detestation of Arabs prevented him from bedding one. Casca, for his part, wanted one of the dark-eyed beauties, but he found himself rejecting each advance. He could not rid himself of the notion that Bethlehem held something for him—some key to his fate, some clue to the way he might eventually be freed from the curse of the religious rebel who had been born here to die on Golgotha. Bedding a woman just didn't feel right under the circumstances.

CHAPTER FIFTEEN

An Arab poked his head timidly from the doorway of his shuttered shop.

"Honorable masters," he whined, "would you care to honor my store by looking upon some rare and exotic treasures not frequently offered for sale?"

They stopped. A faded sign announced: ABU BEN ASID, ANTIQUARY AND RELIQUARY.

"I'll bet he tries to sell us Moshe Dayan's eye patch," Epstein sneered as they moved toward the doorway.

Casca was less concerned with the merchandise than with the possibility of a trap. The wily old Arab might well consider it a good afternoon's work to dispatch a colonel and a major of the conquerors' army.

Casca unlatched the flap of his pistol holster and waved Epstein back to step warily into the store, his eyes searching for trip wires or other signs of a booby trap.

As if aware of his apprehension, the old Arab threw open the window shutters, flooding the small room with light. Still Casca hesitated, allowing his eyes to grow accustomed to the light that now illuminated the Arab's treasures.

And what treasures. Casca recognized immediately the Gladius Imperius Iberius, the Roman shortsword, and alongside it a legionnaire's helmet and leather armor. On another wall was arranged the shield and armor of an English Crusader.

Another wall was devoted to relics of the Great War: rifles of Lawrence's Arab Legion, spent artillery shells, the emu-plumed slouch hat of an Australian light horseman, the helmet and goggles of a downed German flyer. A sign said that the helmet and goggles had belonged to von Richtofen, the Red Baron, whom Casca had good reason to remember had died over France. The fourth wall was covered with swastika flags, Union Jacks, World War II steel helmets, bayonets, Lee Enfield rifles, some pistons salvaged from the Maybach engine of a Panzer 111 tank, and a German officer's cap and jacket with the badges of a colonel general. Another sign said that these had been part of Rommel's uniform.

"Fakes. Fakes. Fakes. Fakes. Fakes," Casca heard Epstein grumbling behind him. "I'll bet you he offers us one of Christ's sandals." The cynical Dutchman laughed mirthlessly.

The old Arab stared in amazement. "You are interested in Christ?"

Epstein winked at Casca. "Yes," he replied archly, "I am a collector of Christian bric-a-brac. What do you have?"

The Arab bowed and waved a hand toward a curtained doorway. "I do not deal in mere bric-a-brac, but please do me the honor of entering this farther room of my humble store." He bowed again.

Epstein was already striding toward the curtain when Casca spoke: "Major, a little more slowly, please. This toothless old Arab may be even better pleased to kill us than to cheat us. We could represent his ticket to Paradise."

Epstein looked with disdain from Casca to the Arab and

back again. The corners of his mouth turned down in contempt for the notion that this old man might represent a danger. But even an army as casual as his observed the protocol of rank and he silently accepted the warning from his superior officer. But the corners of his mouth curved farther downward.

Casca bowed to the Arab: "Pray, lead us to your treasures."

The old shopkeeper inclined his head and walked unhesitatingly through the doorway, holding aside the curtain for Casca and Epstein to follow.

He clapped his hands and a young boy appeared. At a gesture from his grandfather the boy opened shutters to light the room.

The Arab gestured gracefully. The whole room was crammed with memorabilia of the time of Christ. Prominently displayed on one wall was the Spear of Longinus. Casca gave it a cursory glance. It was right for the period, but it certainly was not the spear he had carried that day on Calvary.

There were pieces of "The True Cross," thongs from a whip of the time, pieces of cloth from the robe Christ wore at his trial. Casca was amused to see that the whole of a Roman Centurion's uniform had been assembled and was labeled as belonging to the man who had commanded the squad that had crucified Jesus.

"These look authentic," he said to the storekeeper, and indeed the sandals, leather skirt, breastpiece, and helmet were old enough and of the correct type.

But he smiled inwardly as he recalled the commander of that squad. No centurion, but a mere sergeant. Casca remembered him well as the first of the many men who were to kill him. The sergeant had died in the whore's bedroom, but Casca, to his own amazement, had survived his mortal wound.

"One hundred percent genuine, good sir. If that centurion were to enter this room today, this uniform would fit him."

"He might have put on some weight since those days," Casca said, and realized that indeed he himself had grown much bigger than he had been then. If he were to find his own old uniform, he would burst it apart if he were to try to don it.

"This is all mere trivia," Epstein said sourly. "Do you not have anything that might be worth our while to look at?"

A look of irritation flickered for a moment across the Arab's face. Of course none of the merchandise was what he claimed it to be. He did not for a moment expect that anybody would be stupid enough to believe the lies that he told. But his fakes were good fakes, contrived from genuine articles of the period, or at least carefully crafted copies. Politeness demanded that they not be disparaged. But what could one expect from ill-mannered Jews? Well, they were the conquerors. It must be Allah's will that this rude infidel should afflict him. So be it.

"As your honor pleases," He bowed. "I do have one treasure that would interest a true scholar. But I fear it is above price."

"There is a price for everything," Epstein returned sourly. "First show us the merchandise and then let us haggle over price."

The Arab looked hurt. Haggle? Fishwives at the coastal ports haggled over the price of their wares. Gentlemen did not so demean themselves. In the lengthy process of discussion and flattery and persuasion that accompanied the making of a sale, the price might, perhaps, be modified until two gentlemen came to a mutually acceptable figure. But haggle? Certainly not.

On the other hand, these infidels are the conquerors.

And the only customers. Let us see how Allah wills the outcome. "I have," the Arab announced ceremoniously, "a piece of the true Bible."

Epstein shrugged and started to rise. "And of the True Cross, the Robe, the lash—"

"Aha. Your cynicism shows a wise awareness," the Arab interrupted smoothly. "But please do not allow such wariness to cloud your judgment."

Epstein got up and paced about. "This is all foolish banter. If you do have something to sell, show it to us. I am in no mood for this game of words."

The Arab bowed, and Casca caught a gleam of satisfaction in his eye. He was getting Epstein's goat and so was moving toward control of the negotiations.

"Honorable sir, please do not incommode yourself. You will see for yourself that this fragment of which I speak is genuine. Indeed, I would not even show it to anybody other than a scholar such as yourself. To the fools in the street this scroll of parchment would only be—"

"Scroll of parchment? You have a parchment scroll? Where from? How old?" Epstein's cynical pose fell from him like a discarded cloak. "Show me this parchment."

The boy reentered the room bearing a silver tray on which stood a coffeepot and cups, a decanter and small liqueur glasses, and a plate of sweets. He placed the tray on a low table.

"Please take some coffee, or a little wine," the Arab said, "while I ready this treasure for your inspection. As you might imagine, I do not keep it where it could be easily observed and might be stolen."

He slowly poured cups of coffee while Epstein struggled to disguise his impatience. Casca sat on a cushion by the little table and accepted a cup and sipped at it meditatively.

A parchment scroll? A piece of the true Bible?

Epstein was in haste over the prospect of a choice

collectible. But Casca's very being seethed as he waited to
see the scroll. Was this why he was here? Was he about to
learn something new about the Nazarene? About himself?

The shopkeeper rolled back a rug and knelt to prise up a
floorboard. From the cache beneath he withdrew a battered
thermos flask. He replaced the board, respread the rug,
then seated himself on a cushion by the low table.

He took an appreciative sip of the sweet, black coffee,
spread his hands to indicate the wine and the sweetmeats.

"Will you not honor my humble household by tasting
these refreshments? The wine is forbidden to me by edict
of the Prophet, his name be praised, but I am permitted to
keep it for guests who come to do business."

"To cloud the mind and sweeten the deal," Epstein
sneered, but he tasted the wine and was surprised to find it
good. He smacked his lips and sipped again, but refrained
from congratulating the Arab on its excellence.

"Your camel-driver prophet is of no more interest to me
than the fisherman prophet of the Christians. Nor am I
interested in Abraham or Isaac. I am not a religious man."

The Arab's hand hesitated on the thermos cap.

"Then perhaps this will not interest you. It deals, I am
told, with an obscure reference to Christ's burial party."

Epstein put down his glass. "What it says does not
interest me. I am only concerned with checking its antiq-
uity and authenticity."

Casca sipped distractedly at his glass of wine. The Arab
was doing a superb job of baiting his hook, too good for
Casca's pleasure.

Casca had no doubt that the scroll would prove genuine.
And he wanted it, whatever the price. But the Arab's
leisurely ritual had brought the reluctant Epstein to such a
fevered pitch of anticipation that he was now itching to get
his hands on the parchment.

The antiquarian removed the stopper and shook from the

flask a tightly rolled yellowish scroll. He carefully spread
it on the table, using the wine decanter and some glasses to
hold it in place. It was about nine inches wide and less
than three feet long.

It reeked of authenticity. The fragment had been torn
out of a larger length of parchment, and the text commenced in the middle of a sentence and ended partway into
another. The language was Aramaic, which had still been
the formal language of Palestine at the time of Christ.
Casca had spoken it badly as he fraternized little with the
locals apart from brief liaisons with whores. By the time
he had returned to Palestine in the time of Saladin, Aramaic
had given way to Hebrew. But there were enough words
that he knew for him to get the gist of what was said.

He recognized the words *accursed* and *soldier* and *mother*
and then he realized that the fragment described the moment when he, "the forever accursed soldier," had handed
over Christ's spent body to his patiently waiting mother.

The Dutchman sat back. His pursed lips betrayed the
thoughts that were tumbling through his mind. It was
genuine, not a doubt of it, but he must not let the Arab see
that he believed so.

"An ingenious forgery," the Dutchman said, unable to
refrain from fingering the parchment. He leaned back and
feigned disinterest.

"There are those," the Arab said, as if in agreement,
"who say that the whole legend of Christ, the whole
Christian Bible is but a forgery laid upon the world by—"

"By scheming Jews," Epstein finished for him. "Is that
what you believe?"

The old Arab spread his hands wide. "Good sir, I am
but a buyer and a seller of goods that come to my hands.
The myths and legends that accompany them I pass on as a
matter of interest."

"And what sort of myth accompanies this scrap of

material?'' Epstein snapped. "How do you claim to have come by it?''

"A desert Bedouin brought it to me. He found it in a cave by the Dead Sea.''

"Rubbish!" Epstein shouted, jumping to his feet. "Do you take me for a complete idiot? You have the effrontery to claim that this scrap of garbage is a part of the Dead Sea Scrolls?''

"I make no such claim, effendi. But the Bedouin did say that he found it by the Dead Sea. I believed him and paid him accordingly. It is certainly very old, preserved wonderfully by the desert climate. What it says I do not know. The language is strange to me.''

"If it were genuine you would have long since sold it in London or New York.''

"It would please me greatly to do so, sir. But I am a poor man and could not afford such a journey. And few scholars such as yourself come to my poor store.''

"I'm not going to listen to any more of this garbage," Epstein snapped. "How much do you want for it?''

"For you, effendi, one thousand dollars.''

"*Wha-a-at?* You rotten thief. A thousand dollars! A thousand?''

"Effendi, if I were to tell you what I paid for—''

"I wouldn't believe you. You bet I wouldn't. If there ever was a Bedouin, I'll bet you robbed him just as you're trying to rob me. I'll give you a hundred dollars.''

He took out his wallet and held out a note. "Take it or leave it.''

The antiquarian removed the decanter and began to reroll the scroll. He waved a hand airily about the room.

"If it is your wish to spend a hundred dollars, I have a few trifles said to have belonged to St. Stephen, and part of a dress that may have been worn by Magdalena.''

"Two hundred is my final word." Epstein slapped two bills on the table.

The Arab went on rolling the parchment and reached for the thermos. "For two hundred dollars I could, perhaps, sell you a fragment of the True Cross. It would represent a loss for me, but for such a gracious customer I—"

"Three hundred, damn you. Three hundred and not one penny more."

"Aha. Now, for three hundred"—the scroll was back in the flask—"I have a very interesting relic of the fisherman, Peter. If you would care—"

"The hell with it. I've had enough." Epstein was heading for the door. "Are you coming, Colonel?"

"No." Casca picked up his glass. "I think I'll finish this wine. There are some items here I would like to look at more closely."

"Then I'll see you at the barracks." He bowed ironically to the Arab, his good humor returning. "Good-bye, you old rogue. Don't cheat my friend too thoroughly."

Abu ben Asid returned the bow and was shaking the scroll from the flask before Epstein crossed the threshold. He spread it again on the table, then turned his back and busied himself at some shelves.

Casca pored over the document. He recognized the words of the curse: "Soldier, you are content with what you are, then that you shall remain until we meet again. As I go now to the father, so you shall come to me."

The next phrase he guessed as: "And so it shall come to pass," but then his rusty knowledge of the ancient tongue gave out. He could only discern an odd word, a snatch or two here and there: "in that year," "when all the world." He leaned back on the cushions as Abu turned from the shelves.

"A most interesting piece, Father; do you not have also the beginning or the end?"

"Alas no, noble one. The stupid Bedouin used the rest of the scroll for a most unworthy purpose and would have so used this part too, but then another alerted him to its possible value. If this document were complete it would indeed be beyond price."

"Granted, old one. But incomplete, it is surely not worth much."

"Not much to be sure. From you I ask only one thousand dollars."

Casca laughed. "The same as you asked of the rude Jew who has just left?"

"Your point is well taken, effendi. Your gracious manners merit consideration. For you nine hundred, ahem, and fifty dollars."

"It would please me immensely to purchase this excellent antique from you, but such a price is way beyond my present means. I am but a poor soldier."

The Arab bowed. "Then let us say only nine hundred American dollars. Surely that is within the reach of a colonel in a conquering army?"

"A half-colonel, Father, and I have not drawn pay. Nor have we yet conquered. I would undertake to return another time and try to meet your price, but who can say where the fortunes of war may carry me, or for how long?"

Abu seated himself opposite Casca, settling himself into the cushions like a man ready to sit for a long time. "Perhaps, as a special favor to a brave man, albeit an enemy of my people, I could let this precious item go for eight hundred dollars."

"You are most gracious. Another time and I would gladly pay this price. But just now my purse cannot stretch to even half of that figure. I can pay no more than three hundred and fifty."

"If it would serve, effendi, I would offer to tear the piece in twain and sell you one half, but I fear this would ruin its value altogether. I can see that you appreciate its worth, and I am moved. I will accept a mere seven hundred dollars.''

"Alas, even so, I cannot buy. Four hundred dollars is more than I can afford. I can offer no more.''

"For such a genuine interest as yours, I will forgo my profit. Pay me but six hundred.''

Casca took out his billfold. He withdrew four one-hundred-dollar bills and laid them on the table. "See, my friend, this is almost all that I have.'' He riffled a few other crumpled bills. "Perhaps there is another fifty here. Could you not permit me to buy your treasure for four hundred and fifty?''

The Arab looked at the bills, rolled his eyes to the ceiling as if in prayer, then looked directly at Casca. "I see that you earnestly want this piece. What can I do? I must suffer a great loss, but I will accept five hundred dollars.''

Casca made a show of digging out more bills and added them to the four on the table. "I shall be impoverished for a month, but it is worth it to do business with a gentleman.''

The Arab scooped up the money and handed Casca the thermos flask. "Please roll your treasure with your own hands.''

As if by chance his hand fell upon a small string of beads made of date pips. "And perhaps you will also accept this little gift. These prayer beads are said to have belonged to one Saul of Tarsus who came to be St. Paul.''

Casca accepted the beads and stood. The Arab stood, too, and walked with Casca to the door where he bowed him into the street.

"A thousand thanks, effendi. May you find in the scroll the message you seek.''

Bemused, Casca replied, "Indeed, Father, I do seek a message amongst these words. I thank you for them.''

"A little way down the street,'' Abu said, "toward the

market, you will find a public scribe who may translate it
for you.''

Casca came upon the scribe's place of business on the
sidewalk by the market place. He sat beneath an awning at
a battered desk behind an ancient typewriter, surrounded
by signs in half a dozen different languages: Arabic, Hebrew, Yiddish, English, French, Italian, German. He offered to prepare correspondence, draft legal documents,
compose love letters. One sign proclaimed: ANTIQUE DOCU-
MENTS APPRAISED. Another said: ARAMAIC TEXTS TRANSLATED.
Casca sat on the tiny stool by the desk and spread out the
scroll.

"You want English?" the scribe asked.

"It is my only language," Casca lied.

"Forty drachmas for a translation. Forty more for an
appraisal.''

"Then I shall have both." Casca laid a hundred drachmas on the desk.

The scribe peered intently at the scroll, then picked it up
and held it toward the sun. "Undoubtedly authentic. I
would estimate its age as more than a thousand years,
perhaps two thousand. In the desert this material lasts
forever.''

He looked at it more closely. "Why, this could be a
piece of the Dead Sea Scrolls. Numerous pieces have
turned up since the first findings twenty years ago. Where
did you get it?''

"I bought it from Abu ben Asid.''

"An honest enough trader as antiquarians go. If you
paid anything less than one thousand American dollars you
have made a bargain.''

"What does it say?''

The scribe took the scroll and rolled it from one hand to
the other as he read the small, close script. It was indeed
an account of the removal of Christ's body from the cross,

and of its being carried to the tomb that had been prepared for the rich Pharisee, Joseph of Arimathea.

"And the accursed one shall soldier on through many lives and many deaths, and shall come again unto the land of Israel." Casca was all ears. "And yet again, and still again." A frown began to crease Casca's brow. "But from the curse he shall not be released, not even unto the seventh time he cometh unto Israel."

A long groan escaped from Casca.

"And the time of his release shall by this sign be known . . ."

"By what, man, by what?" Casca shouted as the scribe paused.

The scribe shrugged. "There is no more. The end of the passage has been torn away." He handed Casca his change of twenty drachmas.

Casca let the coin fall and got wearily to his feet. The scribe said something he didn't hear.

"What?"

"Your scroll, effendi. Here is your scroll." The scribe held out the parchment.

"Oh. That? I don't want it." He turned away.

CHAPTER SIXTEEN

"Not even the seventh time?" Casca mused unhappily as he made his way along the narrow street. Somewhere that damned carpenter's boy had used the expression not even seventy times seven. But that had been something about forgiving enemies. In the Nazarene's whole life he had only encountered three: the money changers, whom he had taken to with a whip; Judas, whom he had cursed to hell for all eternity; and Casca, whom he cursed to soldier until he came again.

"Though he may die many deaths . . ." The words were still running through part of Casca's mind as another part dimly registered the soft pad of fast-moving feet behind him. Lost in gloom, Casca had not noticed that his plodding feet had taken him along the crooked lanes of the ancient city. A dog-leg turn in the twisting street had placed him just beyond the mouth of a narrow alley, and out of it had come the scrawny Arab whose knife now pierced Casca's rib cage.

Ali had been born on a dirty rag on the stones of this alley and had lived in it and on it for all of his seventeen years. The street whore who had borne him had vanished from his ken about the time he was weaned. He had learned to steal as naturally as he had learned to walk, but not so well. To be a good thief took some talent and enterprise, and Ali possessed neither. He survived mainly on the charity of other thieves.

A year ago he had been caught in a stupid robbery attempt and had paid for it with his right hand. Since then he had been reduced mainly to begging as the lack of a hand was a severe handicap in the thieving business.

As a beggar he had been no more successful than he had been as a thief. His unclean hand, the one used to clean after defecating, attracted few and grudging coins, and the loss of the right hand marked him for what he was. What he received mainly were curses and blows and kicks.

But of late things had improved. A poor old woman had taken him into her kitchen to give him some eggs, and Ali had thanked her by stealing her only knife—a wretched scrap of hacksaw blade sharpened on a grindstone and bound with twine for a handle. But the crude instrument had enabled him to add murder to his repertoire.

The Jordanian Army had been mobilizing for some time, and every so often a solitary, drunken soldier had stumbled down the alley, seeking even cheaper or more depraved women than the larger streets offered.

Ali's bare feet made almost no noise on the cobblestones, and the force of his rush with his puny weight was usually sufficient to drive the crude blade through the heart of the victim whose back lurched so temptingly before him.

At the first whisper of the footsteps Casca's body, unbidden, had folded into a sideways crouch away from the faint sound. The knife thrust that had been meant for his heart made instead a slash between two ribs beneath his right arm, the Arab's momentum carrying him stumbling

past him to lose both the knife and his footing and fall in a
heap on the cobblestones.

Casca fell onto him, both knees crushing the abdomen,
bursting the spleen, rupturing the kidneys against the stones.

Casca's left hand grabbed the long, lank hair and slammed
the skull on the roadway as the knuckles of his right hand
crushed the Adam's apple.

The scarecrow body kicked spasmodically and its life
was gone.

Casca reached to retrieve the knife, then saw that it was
a worthless thing, scarcely adequate for cutting up dog
meat in the poor kitchen it had been stolen from.

The stump of the Arab's right arm caught his eye.

"Lucky bastard," Casca muttered as he booted the body
aside. "Last thieving done."

Glennon and the others were waiting at the jeep. Epstein
inquired if Casca had been any further impressed with the
antiquarian's merchandise, and Casca answered: "Nah,
just trivia."

Epstein noticed the rent in Casca's shirt, and the dried
blood.

"You were attacked?"

"More trivia," Casca answered, feeling the line of
dried blood where the wound had already healed to a
scratch.

They drove back to the barracks in a mood of near-silent
anticipation, the only conversation being some speculation
as to which front they might next be ordered to.

Moynihan was playing endlessly with the dial of his
radio, but could only raise Radio Jordan.

The Arab station was playing a Hebrew hymn, and this
was followed by an Israeli pop song. Then came the
startling announcement, first in Hebrew, then in English,
and finally in Arabic: "This is Radio Jordan from the city
of Ramallah coming to you by courtesy of the Israeli Army

Corps of Electronic Engineers. We are pleased to announce that this city is now securely in the possession of Israel, as are the cities of Nablus and Bethlehem.

"Citizens of Tel Aviv will be relieved to know that Israel is also in possession of Qalqilyah, and the bombardment of the city and suburbs of Tel Aviv from that quarter is now at an end.

"The city of Gaza and the whole of the Gaza Strip is now secure to Israel. Our troops are also in control of the Suez Canal.

"We can now report that on Monday, Syrian planes attacked a Haifa oil refinery and the Magiddo airfield. In retaliation the Israeli Air Force bombed the principal Syrian airfield near Damascus, surprising many of that base's airplanes on the ground and destroying most of them.

"A Jordanian Air Force attack on Israeli airfields was also repulsed with losses to Jordan of twenty-nine planes.

"Iraqi planes attacked the city of Nathanga and lost seventeen planes in the attempt.

"The Lebanese Air Force has lost a British-made Hawker Hunter aircraft over the Sea of Galilee. A second aircraft managed to escape back to Lebanon.

"Confirmed losses of the United Arab Republic are three hundred and nine planes, including all thirty of their Russian-built Tupolev 16 bombers, and ninety-five MiG 21's. We have confirmed Syria's loss of thirty-two MiG 21's and twenty-eight other aircraft.

"In destroying a total of four hundred and sixteen enemy aircraft, the Israeli Air Force has lost twenty-six planes.

"As a courtesy to our Jordanian audience this station will now resume broadcasting in Arabic."

The last sentence was greeted with hearty laughter from all the men in the jeep.

"Victors can always afford to be gracious," Casca observed.

"Aye," said Moynihan. "Is this war over already, d'ye think?"

"It will never be over," Epstein answered.

When they arrived at the barracks, it appeared that the war might indeed be over. Israeli troops were dancing joyously about, firing rifles into the air, shouting and laughing like boisterous schoolboys.

"Well, Harry went out a victor anyway," Moynihan grunted. He didn't join in the celebrations, but went to his hut and lay on his bunk, playing with the dial of his radio.

Casca knew all too well how he felt and a little later poked his head in the doorway.

"Is this area off limits to commissioned officers?"

A chuckle burst from Moynihan. "Only if they're Protestants."

"Then I'll come in." Casca stepped into the hut. "At last count I qualified as a pagan."

Moynihan waved a hand at his radio. "It's all over, bar the shouting. Bloody long way we've come for a week's work."

"Epstein says it will never end."

"Nor will it—for him. If you want to make your great-grandchildren rich, buy shares in Israeli Air Industries. They're going to be in business for another thousand years." Moynihan stared at the ceiling, not far from tears. "I never thought Harry would've bought it in a corny side-show like this."

Casca searched his mind for the words he knew he wouldn't find. "Mohammed said: 'None falls, even by a killer's hand, until his allotted time be run.' "

"And what the hell would he know?" Moynihan shouted and punched a button on the radio. "Just look at the bloody mess he left behind him."

". . . early reports of the Israeli attack indicate more than a hundred U.S. servicemen killed and wounded," came the steady voice of a BBC announcer. "As yet there is no indication as to what the U.S.S. *Liberty* was doing in the area."

"In South Africa today, the prime minister . . ."

Moynihan was twirling the dial. "What the hell is going on? Maybe I can get Voice of America."

But he could find no other reports and returned to the BBC in time for the headline summary.

"The U.S. Navy's U.S.S. *Liberty*, an electronic intelligence vessel, was detected today fourteen miles offshore from the Gaza Strip and was attacked by Israeli planes and motor torpedo boats inflicting heavy casualties."

Neither Radio Cairo nor Radio Jordan mentioned the incident. Radio Israel also ignored the action, but supplied the news that the Israeli attack on Sharm el Sheikh, blockading the Gulf of Aqaba, had found the fortress deserted by UAR forces.

CHAPTER SEVENTEEN

"What a crazy damn war," Moynihan cursed, and Casca was relieved to see that he had recovered his customary ill temper.

A runner came to the hut to summon Casca to his headquarters. Moynihan hurried with him to the ornate Moorish building that had been the pride of the Arab Legion in Bethlehem.

Orders awaited him that he was to airlift his troops to the West Bank of the Jordan River and besiege the city of Jericho. Airplanes and helicopters were waiting on the nearby airstrip. His orders said that tanks and artillery were already moving into position from Jerusalem and Ramallah and that he was to use these, leaving his own armor and big guns in Bethlehem.

Casca and Epstein studied the battle map while the transfer got underway. To the south of Bethlehem was the Jordanian city of Hebron, still in Arab hands, but surrounded since 1948 by Israeli territory and separated from Jordan proper by the Dead Sea. Hebron and Jericho were the only remaining Jordanian strongposts west of the Jordan River.

"Do you think our guns will be much use here without us?" Casca asked Epstein.

The Dutchman divined his thinking. "I'd rather we had them with us at Jericho. It's less than thirty miles. We could get back here fast enough if the Arabs pushed from Hebron—and I can't see them doing it anyway."

Casca nodded. "Mount up. Take everything that will roll."

Half an hour later Casca was flying over Jericho. The city was entirely surrounded by Israeli troops, armor, and artillery, and more was moving into place every minute.

As soon as his plane landed he summoned Epstein and was pacing up and down before a large-scale map when the major arrived. A pretty Sabra lieutenant was standing by the map wearing headphones and marking up positions as she received the coordinates on the arrival of each new company.

Casca led Epstein to the map. "What do you think?"

The major studied the map carefully for a few seconds, then he pointed a stubby forefinger at the inner circle of symbols. "Mortars?"

Casca nodded.

The finger traced the next circle. "Seventy-five-millimeter howitzers?"

Casca nodded again.

Epstein's finger traced a third circle. "Tanks?"

A nod.

Another circle. "One-oh-fives?"

"Right."

"And one-fifty-fives in the outer ring?"

"Yeah."

A pleased smirk lit the Dutchman's face. "We're going to use proximity fuses!"

"Will it work?" Casca asked.

"Just like Joshua." Epstein roared laughing. "When do we fire?"

"That's up to you. But make it damn soon."

"I'm on my way."

Epstein was already running from the room shouting, "A motorbike! I want a motorbike."

Twenty minutes later he was back by Casca's side, his face florid, panting with exertion, his hair and eyebrows full of sand.

"Every damn gun we've got," he exulted, "is aimed into a box only one hundred yards square. Proximity fuses are set to explode at somewhere around twenty feet up, some a bit more, some less, some on the ground. But, oh Jesus, will it be one big bang."

Casca nodded. "Go to it."

"Yes sir." Epstein started to hurry from the room, then turned and pointed to a slight elevation marked on the map. "This is where I've set up my command post. I will be honored if you would watch with me."

"And I would be honored to do so"—Casca smiled—"but I must attend to the infantry attack."

Epstein snapped to attention like a stormtrooper. "The infantry will not be needed, Colonel."

"I am sure you're right, Major, but overconfidence is an expensive luxury, and one we cannot afford. We're up against the British General Glubb Pasha's Arab Legion, and they may well prove a force to be reckoned with. I trust our men have been warned what to expect?"

"And provided with every possible protection."

The two shook hands as they left the building. Epstein kicked his motorcycle into action as Casca climbed into his jeep. From the floor he picked up a Galil assault rifle and slammed a fresh 5.56-mm magazine into place.

"Let's go, Billy."

They made a quick tour of the battle lines, starting from

the outermost ring of .155s, the devastating American-built Long Toms, and spiraled inward circle by circle until they came to the tanks and infantry waiting just behind the 75-mm howitzers.

From the walls of the ancient city there came an occasional round of exploratory artillery fire. The inner rings of troops were suffering a few casualities, but holding their fire on Casca's orders. Deprived of their air force, the Jordanians had only the slightest idea that they were surrounded, and no impression at all of the mass of arms arrayed against them.

Once more Casca cautioned his commanders what to expect, stressing that neither armor nor infantry were to move until they saw his command jeep go forward.

He put Moynihan and Glennon out of the jeep and moved it on through the inner ring of mortars and then another hundred yards. He placed the protectors over his ears and stood behind the wheel, counting down the seconds.

Expecting it as he was, the gigantic explosion nonetheless shocked him, almost knocking him from his feet. Something like two thousand guns had all fired at once.

He threw up his arm to shield his eyes from an enormous fireball that appeared above the city walls and grew and grew, becoming brighter and brighter, shining like lightning even against the brilliance of the sun.

A gigantic slam of hot, roaring noise, as solid as a battering ram, struck him from above, it seemed, as a shock wave poured out from where all the shells had exploded within the city walls.

The walls bulged out as if inflated, then burst in a flying rain of stone that crashed to the sands ahead of him.

From every point of the compass brutal shock waves rebounded as the expanding air was bounced back from the still air that could not yield way fast enough. Wave after wave rebounded, and Casca stood as if paralyzed, wondering just what was happening.

The scorching desert air was suddenly much hotter, as if
there were flamethrowers playing above his head. Casca
panted like a dog as he struggled to breathe the heated air.
Silence.

Then a horrible, ear-piercing, soul-shaking wail that
burst from thousands of throats within the city walls as the
last breath rushed from bodies that were dying where they
stood, eardrums burst, eyes blown out, stomachs turned to
solid balls of tripe, crushed lungs expelling their last breath
through shattered larynxes.

And then another silence.

It took Casca a few moments to realize that he, at least,
was alive, and another moment to act.

Mechanically, he reached for the starter button and was
relieved to feel the vibration of the engine. But he couldn't
hear it.

He put his hands to his ears. To find the earmuffs. He
dropped them to the seat beside him, engaged first gear,
and, still standing, moved the jeep forward, one foot
toeing the accelerator.

All four tires had been blown out by the shock waves,
but he knew there was no need to hurry. He was not
looking forward to what he expected to see within the
ruined city walls. He steered the jeep around heaps of
rubble and drove into the city.

Everywhere soldiers lay on their backs, empty black-
blooded eye sockets staring into the sun, black trickles of
blood drying where it had oozed from ears and noses.

Here and there a ruin of a man stood, or stumbled
vacantly about. These wrecks had been unfortunate enough
to have been somehow protected from the full power of the
percussive blast, and now were shuddering through their
last sightless, soundless, mindless moments of life. One by
one they were toppling to the ground.

Others, still less damaged, were now starting to appear,

dazed and dying, bleeding profusely from what had once been their eyes.

Casca maneuvered the jeep around these walking wrecks, heading for the military barracks in the eastern quarter of the city, which had been the target point for the blast.

Women and children now appeared in numbers, scrambling like bewildered rats from the cellars and basements where they had taken shelter when the city had first realized that an attack was imminent. They groped their way about blindly, gasping for air with ruined lungs, trying vainly to wrestle with the horror with their shattered minds, wheezing pleas for help through crushed vocal cords.

As Casca sighted the barracks that had been the target point, he heard a lone motorcycle approaching from the opposite direction, and saw Epstein, his big mouth sagging open in horror as his head turned from side to side and his shocked eyes took in the devastation that his guns had wrought.

He shut off the throttle, let the bike fall, and shambled toward Casca, tearing at his hair.

"In the name of the God, Colonel, in the name of all the gods, what have I done?"

Casca stopped the jeep, got out, and walked to meet him. He took him by the shoulders and shook him.

"Pull yourself together, Major, you did a good job."

"A good job?" Epstein stared about uncomprehendingly.

Casca grimaced and struck him hard across the face with the flat of his hand, then grabbed him by the arms and restrained him.

"You did a good job. You carried out my orders to the letter."

"Orders? I was following orders?"

"Yes. My orders. And I have another order for you. You're not needed here now. Get back on that cycle and get yourself to the barracks and turn in."

Epstein muttered: "I don't think I'll be following any more orders."

He shrugged out of Casca's grip and shambled away.

Casca shook his head as he watched him go. "Hope he comes around all right. Good artillery officers are hard to find."

He turned the jeep around to meet his advancing troops, and signaled them to retire. Epstein had been right, the infantry would not be needed.

CHAPTER EIGHTEEN

Casca radioed his report of the fall of Jericho to the Israeli High Command and requested that fresh troops be sent to garrison and administer the city while his troops were allowed a rest within secure Israeli territory. He did not explain that he wanted his own men to have as little contact as possible with the ruin that had been Jericho.

The request for relief was granted, but leave was denied. He was ordered a hundred miles north beyond the Sea of Galilee, to the Syrian border. The regiment was to rejoin the Red general, to be kept in readiness for an escalation of the fighting with Syria, whose long-range guns were harassing the Israeli kibbutzim along the border.

During the night Moynihan came to Casca's tent. "Would ye care to hear the world's view of the latest war news?"

"Sure I would. I'm not sleeping anyway."

Casca reached for the bottle of Jack Daniel's in his foot locker and set it on the small desk, which, with its two canvas chairs, were his only privileges of rank.

The level in the bottle dropped steadily while Tommy went through the motions of searching the short-wave band for news reports.

Every few minutes there was the dull crump of a distant explosion as the guns on the Syrian heights lobbed desultory fire onto the Israeli border settlements.

Neither man mentioned that they were drinking Harry Russell on his way. As good a wake as Harry might have wished for. But Moynihan did find some news, and it jolted both men erect in their chairs.

". . . at 3:20 Greenwich Mean Time a United Nations cease-fire went into effect in the Middle East war between Israel and the Arab nations of the United Arab Republic, Jordan, Lebanon, and Iran."

The radio report was punctuated by a number of explosions from the Syrian guns.

"Some cease-fire," Moynihan scoffed. "Say, they didn't mention Syria, did they?"

Casca was on his feet.

"No, they didn't, and I think that fire is increasing. Let's see what's happening."

They were just entering the HQ tent as a runner emerged on his way to rouse Casca. The whole of the Red general's force had been put under the command of Brigadier General Elazar to attack the gun positions on the Syrian border heights.

General Elazar's detailed battle maps showed an elaborate system of fortifications. Israeli intelligence information revealed that these fortified positions had been substantially hardened with reinforced concrete through the advice and assistance of Soviet experts. The strengthening was such that they could withstand direct hits from either artillery or aerial bombardment. The steep approaches were heavily mined and saturated with antitank obstacles.

General Elazar pointed out the strategic features of the situation. The Israel-Syria border ran roughly north from the Sea of Galilee, along the same line as the Jordan River ran to the south of the sea. Only a frontal attack was therefore possible. An attempt at encirclement of the thirty-mile front would require two fighting detours, each of more than a hundred miles through Jordan to the south and through Lebanon to the north. Neither was practicable, and, in any event, that option had been eliminated by the cease-fire with those nations.

"I asked for your force, General Weintraub," said Elazar, "because I have been mightily impressed with the night actions that you have already carried out. But, on further consideration and discussion with General Dayan, we have decided that such difficult ground can only be tackled by daylight.

"We will have no element of surprise on our side, so let's forget about that. Instead we're going to concentrate all our efforts on total preparedness. Nobody is to move at all until everybody is ready to move—and then we'll all go together.

"We're up against the eighth, eleventh, and nineteenth brigades along the border, two more brigades around El Quneitra, and another two armored brigades, plus two mechanized brigades. I hardly need tell you that if all of these manage to spill down from the heights and into Israel, we stand to lose everything we have gained on all the other fronts.

"Syria is a formidable enemy for Israel. The Syrians have forgotten nothing the British taught them, and they have since learned a lot from the Russians. If we should lose here, we could lose all Israel."

The Red general was allocated the toughest nut of the whole thirty-mile Syrian front, the fortress of Tel Faq'r. Tommy Moynihan dubbed it: "Tell 'em Get lost"

All morning Israeli troops were moving into position along the whole of the thirty miles. By eleven o'clock Casca's regiment was as ready as it could ever be, and the order came to attack at 1130 hours.

Weintraub elected to lead the armored attack while Casca led the infantry. At 1129 the two shook hands in front of their assembled troops.

Casca's grip tightened on his general's hand as he recognized in his eyes the look he had seen so often before. Weintraub knew he was not coming back from this one alive. His lightly armored Bren gun carrier charged away to lead the armor at an oblique angle up the steep escarpment.

Casca waved an arm and started straight up the steep slope of the cliff face into the mouths of the Syrian guns as Israeli artillery opened fire on the defenders ensconced in their concrete fastness and in buried tanks.

The Syrians were having a field day. All around Casca men were falling, mainly officers who, like himself, were out in front of their troops.

He saw Weintraub reach the end of his southern traverse of the slope and turn to lead the armor back to the north. The tanks would cross the face of the slope in front of Casca and his men, but he found scant comfort in this. The slight protection afforded by the armor would be more than offset by the extra fire they would attract.

And so it proved. As the tanks crossed the path of the climbing infantry they came under the fire of the guns that were tracking the armor combined with the already devastating fire that was being poured onto the foot soldiers.

Directly ahead of Casca a Sherman had a track blown off, and the stationary tank was then hit by several high-explosive and armor-piercing rounds. As he climbed Casca watched the steel coffin brew up.

Long tongues of flame darted from the gun ports and observation slits. Inside, Casca knew, any crew that were alive would be trying desperately to open the hatch, which had been jammed shut by the force of the explosions.

He heard the muffled crackle of the first few machine-gun bullets exploding on their storage racks inside the tank. Then the louder bursts as the fire reached the cannon ammunition. There was a mighty, deafening blast as all the rest of the ammunition exploded, blowing the turret hatch high into the air, and with it the charred corpses of the two crewmen who had died struggling with it, their blackened arms, legs, trunks, and heads all flying in different directions. The engine melted in a trickle of aluminum tears that congealed into glistening puddles on the sand. A thick pall of stinking black smoke poured out as the machine died in a final retch of burning oil and rubber.

The following tanks maneuvered around the wreck and moved on to the north. Casca hurried forward, waving his men to follow, hoping to be ahead of the tanks when their zigzag path up the steep cliff-slope brought them back again.

The blistering noon sun baked the infantrymen as they toiled up the slope. Casca pushed himself to move faster and faster, struggling to get ahead of the tanks. His breath came in short gasps. God, how he would love to just lie down and rest.

To his left a young lieutenant colonel did just that as the first burst of machine-gun fire from the Syrian positions tore through his chest. Casca glanced to his right in time to see a major go the same way. In each case a captain raced forward to take over the lead position.

Casca gritted his teeth and forced his protesting legs to maintain their pace.

More and more men were falling all around him. The Syrians now had their range, and on the steep stone slope they could not run fast enough to confuse the gunners.

While Casca's body charged on, his mind surveyed the whole scene and considered the alternatives.

To left and right as far as he could see the escarpment was a mass of swarming troops, and with every yard they advanced more and more men fell. To move to either side would be pointless. The steepest part of the slope was now behind them. To stop would be absurd. To turn and retreat would provide the gunners above with the inviting targets of their slow-moving backs as they ran down the steep slope. And to continue the advance was suicidal. He felt himself tiring, his pace slowing. Panting like a dog, he ran on up the slope as Weintraub's BGC passed behind him, followed by his tanks.

If the armor drew away some action he didn't notice it. The hellfire that they were running into was intense beyond calculation. He was near to despair as he saw Weintraub turn again to lead the armor once more across the slope, this time to pass ahead of the struggling foot soldiers. Weintraub's car crossed only a few yards higher up the slope, and as he passed the Red general stood erect, his red helmet in his hand. He waved it like a flag, urging Casca's men on up the cliff.

A burst of machine-gun fire scythed through his crew and he crumpled beside his dying driver.

From somewhere Casca's trembling legs found the extra strength to rush the few paces forward. As the driver died the BGC slowed and Casca managed to scramble aboard.

A single glance told him that nobody in this car had any further interest in this war.

He jerked the driver's body from behind the wheel, throwing him to the ground. The engine coughed, and he tramped his foot on the accelerator just in time to prevent a stall. But the unsteered car was now heading down the slope toward the advancing infantry who were rushing to get out of the way.

As they moved aside Casca gunned the motor and continued on down the slope. He snatched Weintraub's red battle helmet from the seat and circled it above his head, signaling the tanks to follow him.

He raced slantwise down the slope, the line of armor
following, the Israeli infantry frantically scattering out of
the way.

Once behind the advancing lines of foot soldiers, Casca
turned and raced back across the slope behind the line.
Glancing up the slope he could see that now most of the
Syrian artillery fire was being wasted, pounding the empty
area of the slope where the tanks would have been had
they continued on their path. The now-dispersed infantry
were also taking much less punishment.

A terrible clanking tumult from behind alerted him that
the tanks were not as readily maneuverable as his car. A
Centurion had rolled over and was tumbling sideways
down the cliff, crushing dozens of climbing Israelis as it
rolled. Casca gritted his teeth as he visualized the five men
being tumbled about inside the steel shell. He modified his
course and headed once more up the slope, coming around
in a large circle that would bring him up behind the
infantry. He chuckled in grim satisfaction as he saw
shellbursts exploding uselessly all over the slope as the
Syrian gunners sought to locate their enemy again.

By the time Casca's car had completed its pass across
the slope behind his advancing infantry, the Syrian guns
were reaching for him, and getting closer with every shot.

Instead of turning back across the slope to pass in front
of the foot soldiers, Casca drove almost directly up the
cliff, his maneuver aided by the now-lessening degree of
slope.

Once more the Syrian gunners wasted time and firepower pounding empty ground, and then had to search
again for the Israeli armor.

The gunners directly above were the first to get close,
but, as soon as they did so, Casca changed course again,
this time charging directly across the slope just in front of
the infantry.

Now the close-packed armor shielded the foot soldiers from some of the machine-gun fire, and the confused artillery were still trying to realign their guns to follow the tanks, which were now moving fast as they were no longer trying to climb.

This time when he turned Casca resumed the oblique path up the slope, again confusing the Syrians, and now moving very fast as the slope flattened out toward the top of the escarpment.

From the bottom of the cliff the Israeli artillery stopped firing for fear of hitting their own tanks.

Now the tanks opened fire, and at almost point-blank range some of their shells took effect on the massive fortifications.

Casca turned to drive directly at the enemy fort, halting his car right at the outermost concrete wall.

He clapped Weintraub's helmet on his head and leaped from the car, working the action of his Galil as he moved.

Alongside him the first of the Israeli sappers were already placing explosive charges against the walls while others were cutting their way through the great sausages of barbed wire that protected the gaps in the concrete emplacements. In a few more moments there were holes being blasted through the concrete.

Waves of screaming infantrymen surged forward, suddenly recharged with fierce energy as they found themselves on flat terrain after the grinding climb—and within reach of the enemy who had been plastering them with murderous fire.

Several of the Syrian positions were quickly overrun. The designers of the gun emplacements had not allowed for such a suicidal infantry attack, and now the highly skilled Arab artillerymen found themselves locked in hand-to-hand combat for which they were neither trained nor equipped.

They were, however, good soldiers, disciplined and well led. Every Israeli who made it into the bunkers had to kill several Syrians to get there, and huge numbers of the attackers died in the attempt.

But no Israeli soldier wanted to even think of a retreat down the cliff they had just climbed, and they pushed forward relentlessly. The Syrians fought desperately for every inch they yielded, but inch by inch and yard by yard they were forced to retreat.

Casca caught sight of Atef Lufti, wielding his clumsy *shotel* to murderous effect in the narrow confines of the bunkers. The close combat continued throughout the afternoon, and by sunset there were two Israeli bridgeheads on the Syrian heights.

As darkness fell Casca issued orders to regroup and hold position overnight, bringing all the armor in through the breaches opened in the fortifications.

CHAPTER NINETEEN

Medics had taken the Red general's body from his BGC, and Casca took his red helmet to the burial detail camped just outside the fortress walls. On his way he noticed Atef's silver scabbard gleaming in the moonlight and picked it up for him, wondering that Atef had not already found it. He handed the red helmet to the duty corporal and was turning to leave when the corporal spoke.

"I think we've got the weapon that fits that scabbard."

He led Casca to where Atef Lufti's body lay, the great curved scimitar on his chest.

Casca took up the *shotel* and homed it in its sheath, then stuck it through Lufti's belt and folded his hands over the hilt.

A thought struck him. "What's the casualty count?" he asked.

The corporal shook his head. "Don't know how many dead, but you and an Irish sergeant are the only two of our men who made it through the wall unwounded."

The Syrian defenders had withdrawn, making no attempt to counterattack, and an uneasy quiet settled over Tel Faq'r.

Before first light Casca woke shivering in the desert cold beside Weintraub's Bren gun carrier. Billy Glennon, nursing a bayoneted shoulder, appeared to ask if he needed a driver.

"What about your arm?"

"Oh, I'll hold the wheel in me teeth," Glennon answered.

A large Mercedes-Benz limousine appeared and General Elazar got out of the rear seat, Weintraub's red battle helmet in his hand.

"Wein was one of my very best friends," he said. "I know he would prefer that his helmet go back into battle. It looked good on you yesterday. I'd like you to keep it."

He tapped the crossed swords on the helmet. "I talked with Moshe Dayan by telephone this morning. These swords are yours too. He wants you to lead the attack on El Quneitra, while I hold this position. We expect a counterattack at dawn."

He handed over the helmet, acknowledged Casca's salute, and got back into his car.

Casca stared a long moment at the helmet. "I've never been a general before," he muttered.

"Not surprising, General." Billy Glennon chuckled. "It doesn't usually happen more than once in a lifetime."

Casca smiled, but grimly. "No, I guess not." He slowly put on the helmet.

Moynihan, as usual, had already done half a day's work. He had checked with the burial detail on every man that he had lost; visited every one of his wounded in the field hospital; checked that the numerous walking wounded were, in fact, fit enough to fight again; disguising his concern as always with brutal jokes, scowls, snarls, and even abuse. Now he had inspected his replacement personnel and was checking that every weapon was in order, that every man had all the ammunition he might possibly need and as much water as he could carry.

They moved out before dawn and were on the outskirts of El Quneitra when the sun came up.

More Israeli units had now been diverted to this front, and while Casca led Weintraub's force in a dawn assault on El Quneitra, there were simultaneous attacks from the north near the Lebanon border, and from south of the Sea of Galilee.

The rising sun threw the Syrian defenses into sharp relief, silhouetting the enormous bulk of the concrete fortifications, the huge guns casting long shadows across the edge of the escarpment.

Most of the gun emplacements and all of the buried tanks were pointed at the Israeli kibbutzim below the cliff. Only a handful of fixed guns faced south toward Casca's troops as they moved into position.

Epstein, quite recovered from his shock, urged that all of his big guns concentrate on the southern flank of the fortress while the tanks and self-propelled artillery circle east to attack the fortress in the rear.

Casca readily agreed and left the major in command of that sector while he led the armor and most of the infantry to the principal attack.

Over the past few days large numbers of heavy guns had been moved into the Israeli border villages and these opened fire at the same moment that Epstein commenced his barrage.

There was little prospect that either effort could substantially damage the hardened emplacements, but their bombardment kept the Syrian gunners busy in reply, and distracted them from the threat of Casca's force that was moving toward them from out of the Syrian desert.

Casca's tanks found only a very few guns set to fire in their direction as the possibility of an attack from out of Syria had been discounted by Syria's strategists, and by their Soviet advisers. The conservative Soviets had, however, insisted on a high level of hardening of the fortifications, so that most of the shells of the three Israeli bombardments bounced harmlessly off the thick concrete.

Casca stood beside his car watching the battle through binoculars. It was not at all to his liking. The Syrians were outgunned on two of their three exposed flanks, but although Casca was trading more shells, theirs were having more effect. Casualties on both sides were very low, but the edge was in Syria's favor.

Casca racked his brains and searched his enormous experience for some tactic that might break the stalemate. He repeatedly rejected the only solution that occurred to him—a direct assault on the rear of the fortress by his infantry, relying on the sappers to open breaches in the walls, which could then be further hammered by his tanks, and finally penetrated by foot soldiers.

Every one of his men who had fought his way into the trenches of Tel Faq'r had a wound of some sort, and he was extremely reluctant to ask his troops to suffer through another suicidal effort.

He got into his car and pointed to the rear. Billy started the engine and drove through the lines of tanks to where the infantry waited in their rear.

As they drove along the infantry lines Casca counted and calculated. One batallion of mainly wounded, bruised, and severely battered men from the previous day's battle. And most of his sappers were now raw reinforcements, as the demolition squads had taken the most punishment at Tel Faq'r.

He spotted Moynihan beckoning to him and Glennon headed for him.

"I've got a Syrian radio broadcast," Moynihan shouted. "We've only got a few words of Arabic between all of us, but it sounds crazy. Something about the fall of Hell Cuntra."

Casca took the radio and listened intently. He turned to
Hymie, his radio operator. "Raise HQ Intelligence. See if
they know anything about this." He went back to listening, but although he had some command of Arabic, his
puzzlement increased.

After a few minutes Hymie shouted to him. "HQ can't
work it out, but Syrian radio says that El Quneitra fell at
dawn this morning."

"Who the hell, I'd like to know," Moynihan shouted,
"is shooting at us then?"

Casca glanced toward the fortress, where gray puffs of
smoke were bursting from the walls amongst his tanks,
followed by shell bursts.

"This sure is one confusing war."

"Yeah," Moynihan grunted. "I'm sick of it already,
and it's only just started. If we had—hey, lookee there!"
He broke off to point excitedly in the direction of the
fortress.

From its unattacked eastern end dozens of Syrian trucks
and tanks and foot soldiers were pouring out into the
desert. As they watched the stream turned to a flood.

Hundreds of Arabs, mostly empty-handed and bare-
headed, were running from the fort, jostling each other as
they scrambled away in the wake of their armor.

Their panic grew visibly. Now there were maybe a
thousand men outside the fort and more were pouring from
behind the walls every moment.

Casca leaped into his car, snatched up Weintraub's helmet, and waved it around his head as Glennon gunned the
motor.

"Move out. Move out. Let's go."

Casca reached the wide open gates in the fort's eastern
wall as the last of the deserting troops fled.

"Easy now," he cautioned Glennon, who slowed as
they passed through the gate. "Israelis must have come up

the cliff like we did at Tel Faq'r. Take it real slow. Don't want to get shot by our own men."

But there were no attackers.

And no defenders.

The entire fort was deserted. Casca's tanks were now pouring into the fortress area, and he got out of the car by the HQ building where the Syrian flag still flew from its mast.

Warily, weapons at the ready, they entered the building. Most of the inside doors were open, the rooms empty. Casca booted open a closed door and a startled Syrian corporal leaped to his feet. He quickly raised his hands and backed away from the radio he had been operating.

"What is happening?" Casca demanded in Arabic.

The Arab shrugged despairingly and gestured toward the radio. "I am trying to find out."

The only weapon in the room was a submachine gun leaning against the radio table. Casca picked it up.

"Keep trying," he said as he left the room.

The rest of the ground floor was deserted, a single closed door at the end of the corridor.

Casca kicked it open and roared with laughter.

He was looking into a kitchen where half a dozen army cooks were lying at ease on the work benches, guzzling from bottles.

Casca held out his hand and one of the drunks handed him his bottle of cognac. Casca took a great gulp and passed it to Billy Glennon.

"Carry on drinking," he ordered the cooks in Arabic and reclosed the door.

Upstairs there was only one closed door, and as it led to the front of the building, Casca guessed that it was the command room.

He knocked politely.

"Come in," a firm voice said in Arabic.

Casca swung his Kalashnikov where it hung from his
shoulder, checking that he could quickly fan the whole
room. With his finger on the trigger and Glennon and
Nathan hard on his heels, he pushed open the door.

The huge room was elegantly furnished, a large war
table covered with maps in the center. One wall was
entirely windows, and an officer stood with his back to
them looking out toward the Israeli border. Another officer, a lieutenant, sat at a desk to one side.

The lieutenant stood. The other officer turned and Casca
saw that he was a major general. They saluted each other.

"I don't suppose you speak Arabic?" the Syrian general
said.

"A little," Casca answered, "but I am much better in
English."

"I speak English," the Arab replied. "I trained at
Sandhurst."

"May I have your weapons?" Casca asked.

"Of course." The two officers took revolvers from their
holsters and laid them on the map table.

"I see you have brought a bottle," the general said, and
gestured toward crystal glasses on a sideboard. "Perhaps
we can have a drink. Something else I learned at Sandhurst."

The subaltern brought five crystal brandy balloons and
Casca filled them liberally, emptying the bottle.

"It might be premature and even silly to drink to an
Arab-Jewish friendship," the Syrian general said. "Let's
drink to peace."

"To peace," they all said as they raised their glasses.
The Arab general drained his at a gulp and they all followed suit.

"Morale is a funny thing," the general said, weighing
the empty glass in his hand. "This morning I would have
staked my fortune—more, my life, my soul—on victory
here today. But an army's morale is like a dam wall.
When it breaks there is no holding the flood.

"Damn that fool radio news," he shouted, and hurled the goblet through the glass wall, and a moment later the four others did the same.

The general pressed a button on his desk console, and after a few seconds a drunken voice answered.

"Cooks thrive on defeat," he said to Casca. "They're always the last to desert—after they have emptied the cellars."

He spoke into the intercom in Arabic. "Bring me some cognac, you drunken pig."

In a surprisingly short time there was a respectful knock on the door and one of the cooks shuffled into the room bearing a tray on which were three bottles of cognac. A white towel was draped over his left arm.

Obsequiously he placed the tray on the table and turned to leave. As he passed behind Hymie he drew a large butcher knife from beneath the towel and thrust it through the Londoner's ribs.

The drunken cook giggled like a schoolgirl as Hymie slumped to the floor.

"I've always wanted to kill a Jew."

The general snatched up his revolver and clapped it to the cook's head.

"Cowardly dog," he shouted as he fired. He emptied all six chambers into the cook as he crumpled to the floor.

The lieutenant looked up from where he squatted, Hymie's head cradled in his hands. He shook his head.

The general picked up a bottle, opening it as he crossed to the sideboard. He filled four crystal goblets and carried them back to where the others stood over Hymie's body.

"I trust your comrade was a brave soldier," he said as he raised his glass.

"As good as any I've known," Casca said, and a moment later the rest of the huge window disintegrated as four goblets hit it.

CHAPTER TWENTY

At 7:30 P.M. that night, twenty-seven hours after it entered the war, Syria agreed to a cease-fire. She had lost more than a thousand men and a hundred tanks, forty of which were captured undamaged. Her powerful border artillery, the bane of the Israeli kibbutzim beneath the Syrian heights, were permanently silenced, some destroyed by the artillery bombardment, the rest carted off to Israel.

The Radio Israel report concluded with the message that all short-term soldiers were forthwith relieved of duty, and that all wartime-promoted personnel would now revert to their substantive rank.

The war was over.

"Well, that's the end of a brilliant, short career," Casca said, chuckling. "I guess we're all busted back to private."

"A bloomin' six-day wonder," Moynihan muttered. "That's what I am, a bloody six-day wonder."

He tore the three stripes from his arm.

The celebration of the end of the war was the most restrained one Casca could remember. The Muslim town that adjoined the El Quneitra barracks had plenty of brothels, but no bars, so Casca and his buddies chose to stay within the captured barracks and loot its small cache of fine cognac.

The defeated general and his aide were pleased to join them in their small debauch despite the antialcohol strictures of their prophet. By the time they had consumed the fourth bottle all distinctions of rank, race, and religion had been obscured anyway, and they were just a bunch of raucous veterans on a drunk.

They talked and sang and shouted and even danced.

Wardi Nathan entertained them with a Maori *haka*, a fierce war dance accompanied by vigorous facial expressions of clearly cannibal derivation.

The two Arab officers responded with a Bedouin sword dance, using their British-made Wilkinson military swords.

Moynihan and Billy Glennon danced an Irish jig, and Casca closed the bill with a hambone, a hilarious version of the Dance of the Seven Veils. He didn't let his audience know that he had seen Salome dance the original.

Early the next morning they set out from the fort. The Israeli Army had already deteriorated to the undisciplined rabble whose unmilitary demeanor had helped to seduce the meticulous Arab military into the delusion that they were not good soldiers.

Their notoriously unshined boots were dirtier than ever. Most of the soldiers were unshaven. Their highly individualistic uniforms had been further varied by the addition of various items abandoned by the fleeing Arabs—sword and gun belts and weapons, bandoliers, headdresses.

The ragtag and bobtail army set out for their various hometowns in no particular order, and Casca found that he had been effectively relieved of his general's command by the simple departure of his troops.

He considered himself lucky that his Bren gun carrier had not been taken. It turned out that it might well have

been, but a thoughtful Billy Glennon had prudently immobilized it by removing the rotor button from the distributor.

Casca, Glennon, Wardi, and Moynihan set out along the
line of the Syria-Israel border, heading for the captured
West Bank of the Jordan en route for Tel Aviv. Two
young Sabra officers rode with them.

Nursing a monumental hangover, a disgruntled Moynihan counted his assets, and calculated that even with an
expected victory bonus he would arrive back in Gleeson's
bar almost as broke as he had left it.

Along the way they repeatedly encountered struggling
survivors of the Syrian retreat, and they distributed water
amongst them as they went. Casca was relieved that they
reached the Jordan before their water ran out.

They struck across the desert and stopped at a small dry
oasis for a lunch of dates and figs.

They were lying in the shade of the date palms when the
sudden crackle of rifle fire sent them scurrying for their
weapons and the cover of the BGC.

Casca cursed heartily as he crouched beside the vehicle.
"A hangover will always fuck you up," he said with a
scowl as he recalled that they were carrying little surplus
ammunition.

And the small oasis was virtually surrounded. Every
bullet must be made to count. He thumbed his Kalashnikov
to the semiautomatic mode of fire.

"Well, screw 'em anyway," Moynihan muttered from
under the car. "We've got water and shade, we can hold
'em off forever."

Casca didn't answer. At this season this oasis was dry.
They only had the water in their canteens, and the sun was
still climbing the sky. Very soon their shade would move
away from them.

As he studied the terrain a remote chord of memory
resonated in his mind. He had been here before.

From the River Jordan a now-dry wadi ran into the oasis. In the two thousand years that the desert sands had been shifting, the granite walls of the wadi's canyon had not changed too much. A giant beak of rock that his Roman legion buddies had called "Pompey's nose" still looked like the patrician general's famous snorer.

He looked around until he found what he was looking for—the spot where the dry wadi left the oasis. And when he found it his memory cleared. The opening in the rock still looked like what they had called it in the legion— Salome's Slit.

He nudged the Israeli beside him. "If this gets too bad, we're going to move out through there." He pointed to the slit. "There's a permanent spring down there in the bed of the wadi. We can dig for water."

The Sabra turned a puzzled face to him. "You've been here before?"

"I soldiered out here once—a long time ago."

He was relieved from further explanation by a new burst of firing from their besiegers. The Israeli muttered a curse and the Uzi fell from his hand.

"Oh shit," Casca muttered as he realized that the youth was dead. "These bastards can shoot."

But it seemed that the attackers had only rifles. Each shot came separately, and from good cover, affording little opportunity for response.

One of the tires was shot away with a deafening explosion, then another.

"They're tryin' to lower this chunk of scrap iron onto me bleedin' head," Moynihan complained as he squeezed off an answering shot.

A yelp came from where Wardi crouched near the engine. A chance bullet had nicked a radiator hose and he was being sprayed with hot water.

"No wheels and no water," Casca muttered to himself.
"This is not looking any better." Aloud he said: "What
do you think, Billy?"

The big Irishman fired the shot he had lined up and
grinned at the scream from the edge of the oasis. "We got
no wheels, and we got no water," he echoed Casca's
thinking. "But we don't need 'em. If you guys head out
down that wadi like you said, I can stage a pretty good
diversion, and I'll meet you there. There's a box of grenades on the floor. I've kept it stocked up all the way
through."

Casca laughed and thumped the Paddy on his beefy
shoulder.

"Oh shit, I'm sorry," he said as Billy grunted in pain
from the bayonet wound. "This seems to be my day to
screw up all around."

"We're doin' all right Case," Glennon assured him.

But Casca knew it wasn't true. He had fouled up by
leaving the fortress as if in a country that was really at
peace. And he knew so well that this part of the world had
never been at peace.

He had now caught a few glimpses of their attackers,
and knew that they were Bedouins. There were all sorts of
Bedouins, nomadic farmers and goat herders, camel cara-
vaneers, desert caterers, wandering brigands.

They had fallen amongst the worst of them, a band of
thieves who lived by robbing and murdering at every
opportunity the arid landscape afforded. These desert jack-
als had no loyalty to Syria, Jordan, Israel, nor to any
nation but themselves. They would just as readily have
attacked Bedouin travelers.

"Well," Casca muttered as his shot was answered by
another short scream, "we'll give them more than they
might have expected."

He tapped Billy on the shoulder. "Mount up. Just drive off of us."

As he clambered into the car Glennon unlatched a trenching tool from its clip and handed it to Casca. "You'll need this for the water." He was saying good-bye and Casca knew it.

A second later the motor roared and the BGC lurched away, the flattened tires flapping loosely at the sand.

A hail of rifle fire followed the car, the bullets pinging harmlessly off the armor while the soldiers scored several hits on the Bedouin riflemen.

Then Casca was on his feet, leading the rush for the gulch at the far side of the oasis. As they reached it and ran between the granite walls a few of their attackers came out into the open and raced after them.

Wardi Nathan and the young Israeli officer stopped at the slit and sprayed the pursuers with their Uzis. All but three of them fell, but both Wardi and the Israeli collected lead.

Out in the oasis Billy Glennon was driving the protesting vehicle through the sands to the rear of the circle of Bedouins, lobbing grenade after grenade at where they crouched in cover.

A lot of them died where they were, and a lot more died as they tried to escape by running into the oasis where Casca and Moynihan cut them down.

But at the far end of the oasis the long-suffering engine stalled. Billy Glennon stood on the driver's seat and calmly fired his Uzi one shot at a time as the Bedouins rushed at him.

He accounted for several, but there were too many and they quickly surrounded the car in a human swarm.

Billy had been hit several times, Casca knew, and now he threw his spent Uzi at his nearest attacker.

Casca closed his eyes as he realized what was to come. Glennon bit the pin from a grenade and dropped it casually into the box at his feet as his body was riddled with bullets and the Bedouins clambered onto the car.

There was a brilliant burst of orange and red, a terrible noise, and the car, Billy, and the horde of Bedouins disappeared in a great cloud of dust and smoke.

Both Wardi and the Israeli had now fallen to the ground, and Casca and Moynihan crouched over them.

Wardi looked up at Casca, opened his mouth wide and lolled his tongue out of one corner in the macabre Maori man-eating gesture. His eyes twinkled once and he died. Casca turned to see Moynihan closing the Israeli's eyes.

"You and me and them, General," he said as the three remaining Bedouins ran toward them. He dropped his empty Uzi to the sand.

The biggest of the attackers was one of the largest men Casca had ever seen, enormous by Arab standards. He was roaring like a maddened bull as he came firing from the hip; then he threw down his rifle in disgust as it jammed. The two Bedouins running beside him threw away their empty weapons, too, and drew long, curved knives.

Casca dropped his empty gun and his arms moved fast as he blocked the two knife blows that came at him. From the corner of his eye he saw the giant and Moynihan grappling. Casca had blocked one knife blow with a downward swinging curve of his left arm, and the other with an upward circle of his right. He continued the circle around until the Bedouin's arm was locked inside his, and grunted in satisfaction as he heard the bones break.

He swung a heavy boot into the balls of the first attacker, then chopped the maimed one in the neck.

His second mighty kick caught the sagging Bedouin in the throat and then he turned to jump with both heels onto the other's kidneys.

He heard a crack and a horrible scream and turned to see the giant break Tommy's back across his knee. He hurled the small Paddy's broken body at Casca and followed it fast. Casca caught Tommy and held him for a brief moment, the flat of his foot stopping the giant Bedouin in mid-rush as it caught him in the belly.

Casca turned and stopped to lower Tommy to the sand and as the Bedouin rushed again, he caught him with a high backward kick that sank his heel deep into the giant's groin. As he turned back his flailing arm struck the Bedouin mightily in the throat, and he grabbed him by his mangled balls with one cruel hand while the other gouged his eyes from their sockets as he slowly cracked the giant's spine across his knee.

He dropped the body to the sand and walked to where the trenching tool lay on the sand. He placed its edge against the writhing Bedouin's throat and slowly leaned on it, exerting more and more pressure as the artery burst in a fountain of red blood, then the spine was severed, and finally the head was separated from the huge body.

He turned to kneel beside Tommy.

The little man seemed even smaller. He grinned up at Casca.

"The old story, Case, a good little one and a good big one."

"Not that good, Tommy, he's dead."

"So am I, General."

"Rubbish, you're good for a lot of fights yet."

Moynihan closed his eyes wearily. "Ye're a good general, Case."

"That's not such a great trick, Tommy. Generals get lots of help. You're a damned good sergeant."

A crooked grin lifted a corner of Tommy's mouth, one eye opened a slit, and he was gone.

Casca smoothed the eyelids closed and picked up the trenching tool.

He dug long and deep and wide, and laid the two young Israelis, Wardi, and Moynihan side by side.

At the last moment he placed Weintraub's red helmet over Tommy's face.

"To keep the sun out of your eyes, old son."